Hazel & Griffin

THE MYSTERY OF THE WITCHING FLOWER

ATTICUS BLACKWOOD

Contents

Chapter One
New Beginnings

As I looked out the window during our long drive from New Mexico to Washington State, I couldn't help but admire the stunning mountain range that stretched before us. The view was so breathtaking that I could easily stare at it for hours. With my Mom and younger brother Griffin by my side, we had a lot of fun exploring all the sights along the way. It was an excellent opportunity to bond and create new memories together.

As we journeyed on, I occasionally glanced at my reflection in the rearview mirror. I saw my curly black hair and tanned skin, which glistened in the sunlight that poured in through the sunroof. Though I wasn't thrilled with my scrawny figure, I accepted it for what it was. Meanwhile, my younger brother, Griffin, was seated in the back, engrossed in his Nintendo Switch as he played Pokemon. With his short black hair and tan skin, he looked much like me but was shorter and slightly overweight. Being only thirteen, I knew he still had much growing to do.

As for me, I felt like I had already reached my peak, just like my Mom. At seventeen, I knew I had inherited her beautiful looks and assumed that's what I would look like for the rest of my life. I didn't mind it, though, as my Mom was stunning. However, she often remarked that my brother and I looked like our late father, even though Griffin resembled him more with their similar features. Unfortunately, my Dad passed away in a construction accident last year, leaving us with a generous life insurance policy that provided us with more money than we could ever imagine. With it, my Mom could move us anywhere in the United States and pay for our college tuition.

Before this journey, we lived in a run-down neighborhood riddled with crime. But we had each other, which made everything okay. In fact, due to all the crime, I became somewhat of a social media detective. My Dad and I enjoyed watching crime shows and reading detective novels together, which inspired me to solve mysteries and help people find closure. I would document everything on social media, from lost car keys to stolen bikes, and even help someone recover their stolen car. My following grew so large that even the local police began to follow me.

Now, we are starting a new chapter in our lives. My brother would start high school, and I would finish my last year with most of my credits already earned. I would only need to attend three classes daily, giving me plenty of time to spend with my Mom. She had always been there for us, working two jobs to make ends meet and provide for our family. She dreamed of opening her flower shop, a pipe dream since childhood. Unfortunately, life never gave her the chance to pursue it until my Dad passed away. He always encouraged her to follow her dreams, and she finally had the opportunity to do so. We were moving to Washington State, where the best flowers were grown, and it was much safer than where we were coming from. Looking at the mountain range again, I knew this was the right move for us. It was a new beginning and a chance to start fresh, leaving behind the pain of our past and embracing a brighter future.

As we were driving towards our destination, my younger brother asked my Mom how much longer it would take to get there. My Mom replied that we were almost there and about to reach a small town called Pinecrest Fall. She described it as a quaint little town with a bustling downtown area home to many small businesses that had flourished and succeeded without any interference from big corporations.

When I asked my Mom why she had chosen to open a flower shop in the center of downtown, she explained that she had done extensive research before purchasing the shop. She had deliberately chosen a location flanked by a bakery and a pottery shop so that customers could buy flowers from us, a pot from the neighboring shop, and even grab a snack all in one go.

When my brother asked why we had bought a house outside of town, my Mom explained that we had lived in a cramped space for most of our lives and that she had wanted to buy a place with plenty of space. She had also found that the older houses on the outskirts of town were significantly cheaper than those closer to the town center.

As we approached the town, my Mom pointed out a big green sign that read, "Welcome to Pinecrest Fall," adorned with beautiful paintings of pansies. We passed two exits to the house - one led downtown and the other to Evergreen Lane. My Mom turned onto Evergreen Lane, and we began our journey down a long, wooded road. We passed several old-school vintage houses, all looking like they were built in the 1800s.

Finally, we arrived at our new home. From a distance, it looked just like the pictures my Mom had shown us online, but we were eager to explore it in person. We pulled over on the side of the road since the driveway was filled with movers. We got out of the car and looked at our new home.

Every detail captivated me as I stood mesmerized by the grand two-story Victorian-style house. The exterior walls coated in a light blue hue brought the stunning clarity of a bright, sunny day to mind. The white trim surrounding the windows and doors gleamed in the warm sunlight, adding to its already impressive beauty. The roof, amalgamating

A-frames and a sizeable conical roof was a sight to behold. The dark charcoal grey color of the roof reminded me of the glowing embers in a fire pit, and its prominent position in the front and center of the house made it all the more captivating.

As my gaze shifted toward the wrap-around porch, I was greeted by the sight of cream-colored pillars that added an air of sophistication and elegance to the already impressive structure. The large windows around the house were so expansive that they seemed like doors, and one could easily walk through them. The front yard was a testament to the owner's love for nature, with various ground cover plants, a few bushes, and a couple of pink hydrangeas adding splashes of color, creating an inviting and peaceful atmosphere. The mountain hemlock tree that overshadowed the house provided a much-needed respite from the heat, and its towering presence added a sense of tranquility to the already serene environment.

I couldn't help but notice the cream-colored gravel driveway leading up to the house, which contrasted beautifully with the sky-blue house. Every aspect of the house was meticulously planned and executed, creating a perfect blend of beauty and harmony. Overall, the house was a breathtaking sight, and it was evident that every detail was carefully thought out to make it an inviting and harmonious space.

As we were standing outside, my brother asked my Mom if we could go inside the house, and without any hesitation, she said, "Of course, you can." We both looked at each other and quickly raced up the driveway. Our excitement was because we had made a bet earlier, and whoever got to their desired room first would be theirs. I was determined to get the best room before my brother got there. As we navigated through the movers and their boxes, we raced up the porch steps, our hearts pounding excitedly.

Upon opening the door and stepping inside, I was immediately transported back. The entrance led into a grand hallway that seemed to stretch on endlessly. The walls were adorned with yellow wallpaper and pink flowers, giving it a truly vintage feel. As I walked further into the hallway, I couldn't help but be struck by its spaciousness. The floor was covered by a huge rug, one of the most exquisite designs I had ever seen. The center of the carpet was adorned with multiple red, white, green, blue, and pink flowers, all arranged neatly in a rectangle. This beautiful centerpiece was surrounded by an elegant red frame with red, white, and blue flowers. The hardwood floors shone brightly under a magnificent chandelier that hung in the center of the hallway. The chandelier was a work of art with numerous glass crystals that beautifully reflected the light. At the end of the hallway, I could see double white doors that must have led out to the backyard. On the other side of the hall, a staircase led up to the second floor. The stairs were covered with a rug with the same exquisite design as the rug on the floor, giving the hallway an elegant and cohesive look.

As I turned to the right, an awe-inspiring grand doorway appeared, leading to a spacious living room that seemed straight out of a fairytale. The room was colossal, with a high ceiling in the sky adorned with intricate designs that added to its elegance. The walls were painted in a charming shade of pink, reminiscent of cherry blossoms in full bloom. The contrast with the intricate white floor designs created a harmonious and captivating atmosphere.

The massive windows were pushed out, creating a cozy little cove where one could sit and gaze outside, marveling at the picturesque view. The sunlight pouring in from the windows illuminated the room, perfectly highlighting the intricate details that enchanted it.

On one side of the room, I noticed an old wooden cabinet crafted by hand. Every little detail etched into it was a testament to the artisan's skill and dedication. On the opposite side of the room, a large brown leather sofa was positioned right next to a magnificent stone fireplace, exuding a cozy warmth that filled the air. The fireplace had pillars that held up a ledge filled with old candles, creating a mesmerizing ambiance that was nothing short of magical. Above it was a giant mirror with a gold frame that held it in place, adding to the room's grandeur.

Lastly, at the back corner of the room, I saw a beautiful wood piano with bright white keys and a music stand next to it, allowing one to read music as they played. The piano's wood finish was a sight to behold, with a lustrous sheen that reflected the light in the room, making it seem glowing. My fingers itched to play a tune on it, and I could almost hear the music resonating through the room. The living room was a masterpiece, and I couldn't help but feel lucky to witness its grandeur.

To my left was a spacious dining room that welcomes you. The walls are painted solid sky blue, giving off a serene and peaceful vibe. A large wooden table with six matching chairs occupies the center of the room. The table looks sturdy, and the chairs are spaced around it with enough room for people to move around comfortably. The table is adorned with a lovely white tablecloth, which has intricate designs of cherries scattered all over it, adding a touch of elegance to the room.

One side of the dining room boasts a large window with wood trim, allowing natural light to flood. The light illuminates the room with warmth and creates an inviting atmosphere that beckons you to step inside. A simple candle-like chandelier made from gold hangs from the ceiling, adding a touch of sophistication to the ambiance.

Moreover, a beautiful china cabinet is placed next to the kitchen door, displaying fine china and silverware that give the room a higher-class feel. The cabinet is intricately designed and well-lit, showcasing the elegant collection inside. It is a piece of art and adds to the room's beauty. The dining room is a perfect blend of style and functionality, making it ideal for family and friends to gather and enjoy a meal together. It exudes warmth, elegance, and sophistication, making anyone feel at home.

As I followed my brother racing up the stairs, I couldn't help but feel a sense of excitement and anticipation building up inside me. However, my enthusiasm was short-lived, as my brother quickly reached the top of the steps and slammed the door shut, claiming the room for himself. Undeterred, I turned and entered the first room I saw, and its sheer grandeur immediately struck me.

As I stepped into the room, its beauty instantly struck me. The space seemed to stretch on forever, with high ceilings that made me feel like I was in a palace. My eyes were immediately drawn to the center of the room, where a magnificent crystal chandelier hung, casting sparkling light in every direction.

But it was the bed that genuinely took my breath away. It was the most enormous bed I had ever seen, covered in soft pink pillows and a luxurious gold-spun bedspread adorned with delicate flower designs. Above the bed, a pink curtain cascaded down, adding to the regal ambiance of the room.

On the right side of the bed, a small mirror hung on the wall, reflecting the opulent setting. Underneath it, an elegant white desk and matching chair beckoned me to sit and admire my surroundings. Across from the bed was a massive vintage cabinet adorned with intricate gold floral designs that seemed to be etched into the wood.

The enormous window on the far wall allowed a flood of natural light to pour into the space, illuminating every corner of the room. It was almost blinding, but I couldn't help but feel grateful for the light that breathed life into the space. I knew I had to find some curtains to help dim it more comfortably. Overall, I was stunned by the sheer luxury and beauty of the room. No expense had been spared in its design, and I couldn't wait to personalize it and make it my own.

As I stepped out into the hallway, I caught sight of my brother emerging from his room. I couldn't help but ask him, "How do you like your room?" He looked at me with a wide grin and responded, "I love it! It's enormous - almost the size of our old house - and there's so much space that I don't even know what to do with it all."

"I know exactly what you mean," I replied, still looking around in disbelief at the sheer size of our new home. "It feels like a palace in here. There's so much room that I feel like I can finally stretch out comfortably." Suddenly, Griffin's attention was drawn to a door at the end of the hallway. "Hey, where does that door lead to?"

he asked, pointing eagerly. I was just as curious, so we decided to investigate together.

As we opened the door, we were met with a narrow flight of wooden stairs that seemed to lead up to the attic. We climbed the steps without hesitation, eager to explore this new part of our home. Finally, we reached another door with a half window above it adorned with a spider web design.

As I turned the doorknob, the old wooden door creaked open, and I stepped into the vast and airy attic. The walls were stripped down to their bare wood, devoid of wallpaper or paint. My gaze was drawn to the three large windows that covered the entire wall, letting in ample natural light and offering an unobstructed view of the stunning scenery outside. A beautiful vintage wooden chair was positioned before the windows, beckoning me to sit and bask in the sun's warmth.

As I walked further into the room, my attention was immediately drawn to the grand table in the center of the attic. The table was large enough to accommodate eight people comfortably and was surrounded by matching wooden chairs, each with intricate carvings. A beautiful black chandelier hung above the table, with candle-like lights and black hoods covering each, creating a cozy and inviting atmosphere.

In one corner of the room, I spotted a round wooden table with some books and a wooden chair pulled up to it. The cozy nook looked like the perfect spot to curl up with a book and immerse myself in the peacefulness of the attic.

Overall, the attic was spacious enough to comfortably accommodate twenty people, yet it still felt cozy and inviting. The combination of vintage and modern elements gave the space a unique and charming character, making it a perfect place to unwind, relax, and feel at home.

As my brother and I walked into the room, we couldn't help but feel a sense of excitement. The room was spacious, with large windows that let in plenty of natural light. We looked around, taking in every detail of the space. My brother was the first to speak, "This room is perfect," he said, a smile spreading across his face. "Perfect for what?" I asked, curious as to what he had in mind. "For our detective office, of course," he replied with a glint in his eye.

It wasn't the first time my brother had expressed an interest in mystery-solving. Ever since our Dad passed away, he had been increasingly drawn to solving puzzles and uncovering secrets. I wasn't sure if it was his way of coping with the loss or if he wanted to feel closer to our Dad by pursuing something he was passionate about. Whatever the reason, I was happy to have a partner in crime-solving.

As my brother continued to explore the room, I found myself a chair and sat down, watching him with amusement. He was like a kid in a candy store, examining every nook and cranny of the space. "You want to make this room our headquarters or something?" I asked him, trying to hide my excitement. "It's the perfect room for us, and we can get a whiteboard and some more supplies to help us figure out what's going on."

I couldn't argue with that. The room had a certain charm, and I could imagine us spending hours pouring over clues and brainstorming solutions. But I couldn't help but voice my concern. "Okay, but what if there is no crime here?" I asked, not wanting to sound hostile but genuinely curious. After all, we had only seen the movers during our time in the house.

My brother turned to face me, a mischievous grin on his face. "No matter where you are, there is always a mystery around every corner. Or at least that's what Dad used to say." I smiled at remembering our Dad's

love for solving puzzles and mysteries. He had instilled a sense of curiosity and an eagerness to explore the unknown.

Feeling a surge of emotion, I got up from my chair and walked over to my brother, giving him a tight hug. He tried to act like he didn't want one, but I knew he needed it. We may not be the Hardy Boys, but we were a team, and together, we could solve any mystery that came our way.

As we descended the stairs, we were extra careful not to bump into the movers carrying boxes and furniture up to the second floor. Our move from New Mexico wasn't much, but my Mom had ordered plenty of new items to make our new home feel cozy. She spent hours browsing online for new furniture and artwork to fill up the empty spaces in the house. As we reached the main hallway, we walked through the dining room, where a large wooden table surrounded by chairs sat at the center. We could smell the freshly baked cookies in the air, which meant my Mom was probably in the kitchen. Despite being skinny, she always loved eating and often snacked throughout the day. As we headed towards the kitchen, we could hear the faint sound of her humming a tune, which meant she was in a good mood.

As I stepped into the kitchen, I was awestruck by its grandeur and spaciousness. The cabinets, painted in a rich hunter green, were expansive and wrapped around the entire kitchen, providing ample storage space for all cookware and utensils. The white marble countertops were stunning, adding a touch of elegance and sophistication to the space.

I approached the sink and noticed it was right before a set of French windows. The bright sunlight streamed into the room, highlighting the white porcelain sink basin. The view outside was breathtaking, with the garden's lush greenery and colorful flow-ers creating a picturesque backdrop.

The silver stove on the other end of the kitchen was a true master-piece. It was a six-burner stove with double doors at the bottom, mak-ing it perfect for cooking large meals. The stove was positioned directly in front of a stunning white brick back-splash, which added texture and con-trast to the otherwise smooth sur-faces in the room. The combination was both striking and functional.

In the center of the kitchen stood a massive kitchen island. Its wood-en legs perfectly matched the color of the cabinets, making it blend seam-lessly with the rest of the kitchen. The island had the same white marble countertop as the rest of the kitchen, creating a cohesive look. Four wooden stools around the island provided a comfortable place to sit and eat. My Mom was sitting on one of the stools, holding a plate of freshly baked chocolate chip cookies that filled the air with their sweet aroma. It was a warm and welcoming sight that made me feel right at home.

"Hey kids, have you picked out your rooms?" my Mom asked excitedly while munching on a delicious cookie. We had just arrived at our new home and were eager to get settled in. My brother, Griffin, and I looked at each other, grinning from ear to ear.

"Yes, we have. We even found the attic space, which will be our detective's office," Griffin replied, reaching for a cookie as well.

"That's fantastic! We'll have to get you some supplies so you can set up your base," my Mom said, her eyes sparkling with joy. She always encouraged us to pursue our interests and passions. "I can't wait to add my personal touches to my room once the movers are done," I chimed in, grabbing a cookie too.

"The movers won't be long, so I baked some cookies for them. After they're done, we'll head to the flower shop and then to city hall to pick up my business license," my Mom said, taking another bite of her cook-ie. Suddenly, we heard some noise outside and looked out the window to see three kids playing basketball across the street at a red Victorian house with a white roof. "Oh, look at that. More kids. Maybe you should go and introduce yourselves and make some friends," my Mom suggested, turning back to her cookies.

I was hesitant to make friends, as I was always shy and reserved. But my brother wanted to go and meet the other kids, so I turned to my Mom and said, "Okay, let's go meet our new neighbors. Just let us know when you're ready to leave, Mom." She nod-ded, her mouth still full of cookies.

Griffin and I stepped out of our house and saw the kids playing across the street. We made our way towards them, our steps quickening with enthusiasm. As we reached the driveway, we saw three kids taking turns throwing a basketball into the basket. Griffin's face lit up with excitement, but I took the lead to introduce ourselves.

"Hello, I'm Hazel, and this is my younger brother Griffin. We just moved in next door," I introduced, my voice friendly and welcoming. The eldest of the group turned around, surprised, and waved us over. "Hey there, Hazel and Griffin. I'm Miles," he spoke, extending his hand towards us.

Miles was a towering figure, slim and tall, with sandy red hair and freckles that dotted his face. His arms were pale, almost translucent, as if they had never seen the sun. But what stood out the most were his piercing blue eyes, which shone brightly against his fair complexion, starkly contrasting his siblings' green eyes. Lucas, Miles' younger brother, looked like a miniature version of Griffin - short and chubby, as if he was still growing into his body. He had vibrant red hair and slightly tanner skin than Miles. The youngest of the trio, Ava, was petite and had bright orange hair tied up in adorable pigtails. Her size and demeanor suggested she was around five or six years old.

The basketball court was an impressive sight. It was a small, makeshift court assembled in the front yard of Miles' house. Next to the hoop, there were a few chairs and a cooler with drinks and snacks. The court was surrounded by a fence on one side, while a dense line of bushes bordered the other side. The relatively quiet street was lined with trees that provided ample shade, making it an ideal spot to play. As Miles continued chatting with us, Lucas and Griffin exchanged glances as they sized each other up.

On the other hand, Ava seemed content watching the older kids play.

Lucas and Griffen were playing a one-on-one game game while Miles, Ava, and I were chatting. Miles was curious to know why we had moved to Pinecrest Falls. As Lucas scored a basket on Griffin, I replied, "We moved here from New Mexico. My Mom purchased a shop downtown and plans to open a flower shop soon." Ava's eyes sparkled with excitement, and she exclaimed, "We're getting a flower shop!" Miles smiled and added, "Looks like it. It's the last missing piece this town needs." They both seemed thrilled, which was reassuring since my Mom had researched extensively before making this move.

I was curious to know if Pinecrest Falls had ever had a flower shop before, to which Miles replied, "We had one a few years ago, but the owner retired, and no one has opened one since. It's a small town, and most people here either own a shop or work on one of the few large farms around here. Our Dad is a rancher, and our Mom is an inspector for chicken houses. So, I guess your Mom is in the shop owner category. What did your Dad do?"

I hesitated for a moment before responding, "My dad passed away two years ago, and we moved here for a new start." Miles expressed his con-dolences, adding, "This town might be small and old-fashioned, but it's a great place to live. You guys will love it." However, Lucas interrupted Miles, saying, "Well, except for the missing kids." He had just finished playing basketball with Griffin, and both of them were drenched in sweat with big grins on their faces. I was immediately concerned and asked, "What missing kids?"

Miles seemed to be frustrated with Lucas and told him to stop, saying, "That has nothing to do with us wel-coming our new neighbors." But I was interested and wanted to know more, so I asked them to tell us more about the situation. However, my Mom interrupted us, calling out from our new house, "Hey, Kids, it's time to go." As we walked back to the car, Miles, Lucas, and Ava waved goodbye to us and said they would talk to us later. Griffin and I exchanged knowing looks, and I said, "It looks like we got our next case."

I couldn't help but take in the picturesque surroundings as we drove into town. The drive was charming, with abundant scenic views along the way. We passed by several charming dairy farms and apple tree farms, which added to the beauty of the journey. After a short while, we saw a sign that read "Welcome to Downtown," which signaled our arrival at the edge of town. We turned onto Whispering Pine Lane and continued straight, passing by a row of red-brick buildings that were stacked closely together, interspersed with small alleys. People were bustling around, going in and out of quaint little bars, clothing boutiques, and coffee shops. The atmosphere was lively, and everyone seemed to be in high spirits, ready to indulge in some retail therapy.

As we continued, we spotted a few bronze statues we didn't recognize, but we assumed they were of some historical figures. We also passed by a grand building with a golden dome on top and statues of eagles on each corner. The building looked ancient and significant, as if it were a museum exhibit. Above the glass doorway, in bold, bright gold letters, read the words "City Hall." It was then that we realized that we would have to head there after we were done at the flower shop.

Finally, my Mom turned the car down Jubilee Avenue, made another right turn, and pulled the car up in front of an empty building with a bakery on one side and a pottery shop on the other. Both had unique signs above their doors. The bakery's sign was a big blue rectangle with gold lights around pink letters that spelled "Evelyn Baked Goods." The pottery shop's sign was in the shape of a flower pot and was royal green, with yellow letters inside the pot that read "Lily's Pottery Barn." On the other hand, our building had no sign yet, and the windows were covered in black paper to keep prying eyes away. My Mom parked the car right in front of the building, and we all got out, feeling excited and relieved to have finally made it.

As we approached our new building, my mother's apprehension was palpable. My brother and I tried to comfort her by placing our hands on her back, offering our unwavering support. She opened the door with a smile, and we all stepped inside our flower shop for the first time. To my delight, the interior surpassed my expectations. The store was bright and airy, thanks to the large windows positioned in the center of the building. Passersby could easily see inside and catch a glimpse of the beautiful flowers and arrangements. In front of the windows, small white shelves lined the walls from end to end. I could already envision my mother adorning them with stunning floral displays to entice potential customers. Both side walls were identical, featuring shelves attached to the wall, starting from the bottom and stretching to the ceiling. These shelves provided ample space to showcase a wide variety of flowers and other plant materials. The floors were well-polished, shining hardwood, making the store look even more inviting. In the center of the store stood a large wooden table with shelves on either side, which could be used to showcase the most beautiful floral arrangements. The back wall featured wooden shelves extending from the floor to the ceiling, providing additional space to display flowers and other decorative items. In front of these shelves was a large wooden table with a white marble countertop -

the perfect spot for our cash register. Overall, I was thoroughly impressed with the store's layout and design, and I couldn't wait to see it filled with breathtaking flowers.

The space was already filled with potential, and I couldn't wait to see what it would look like once we added flowers and plants to the mix. My Mom walked over to the counter, her hands smoothing over the surface as if she were trying to take it all in. A smile graced her face, one of pure joy that made my heart swell with happiness.

I turned to my brother, who was already taking stock of the space and looking for things to clean. "What should we get started on first, Mom?" he asked, eager to get to work. "We don't have any flowers yet, but we can at least get the place cleaned up a bit." But my Mom had other plans. "We will get to all of that in due time," she said, taking a seat behind the counter. "But first, we need to head to city hall so I can get my license and any other paperwork I might need to fill out."

As she spoke, I could see the excitement and nerves battling within her. This was now her flower shop, and the reality of it all was starting to sink in. But I knew she was more than ready for this new adventure, and I couldn't wait to see where it would take us.

A sudden loud knock on the door distracted us from our conversation, causing us to look in the same direction. We were curious to see who it was, so we peered through the glass window and noticed two elegantly dressed ladies standing outside, waving at us excitedly. The first lady was tall and slender, with a beautifully styled short brown afro that complemented her caramel complexion and bright brown eyes. She wore a denim shirt, brown khaki pants, and a brown apron with "Evelyn" printed on it. The second lady, who was older, had silver-white hair that was neatly tied back and flawless tanned skin that hinted at her love for the sun. She was wearing a blue long-sleeved shirt, black pants, and an olive-colored apron marked with clay stains. Their appearance clearly indicated that they were our new business neighbors.

As my Mom walked towards the door, she took a deep breath and composed herself. She opened the door with a warm smile and greeted the two ladies standing outside. "Hello, my name is Olivia, and these are my children Hazel and Griffin. Would you please come on in?" she said, extending her hand to welcome them in. The ladies walked into our shop, their faces beaming with excitement, and introduced themselves. The lady with the apron that read 'Evelyn's Bakery' was actually Evelyn herself, who owned the bakery next door. The other lady was Lily, the owner of the pottery barn. "How are you all settling in?" Evelyn asked in a friendly tone, placing a box of freshly baked chocolate chip cookies on the center display table.

Griffin, my younger brother, did not hesitate to grab himself a cookie. My Mom shot him a look, reminding him of his manners. "I'm sorry, but the cookies smelled so good. Thank you for the cookies, Ms. Evelyn. They are delicious," he said, putting down the cookie and looking apologetic. "Don't worry about it, Griffin. I would have done the same if it was my first time having Evelyn's cookies," Lily said, grabbing a cookie for herself.

I walked over and took a cookie for myself, savoring the warm, gooey texture and the rich, chocolatey flavor. "How is it running a bakery and pottery shop here?" I asked, curious about their experiences. "This town is great; there is no big corporation to shut us out, and there are plenty of people around for everyone. It's a real community that you won't see anywhere else," Evelyn said, smiling with pride.

"Downtown picks up after five o'clock. Most of the people who live here work on farms in the surrounding area, and they all get off around five o'clock. The streets will be packed in a couple of hours," Lily added. "Well, that's good to know. I hope the people like flowers," I said, feeling optimistic about our new flower shop. "People have been wanting a new flower shop ever since Sam retired and closed hers down a year ago. You guys got here just in time," Evelyn said excitedly.

"Well, that's even better. It looks like we are going to be fine after all," my Mom said, her face brightening with hope. We all sat around, sharing stories and explaining more about why we moved to Pinecrest Falls. The conversation flowed easily, and we felt a sense of belonging and connection with the two ladies.

"Oh, look at the time. We got to get over to city hall. It was nice to meet you ladies, but we got to go," my Mom said, interrupting the conversation. "No worries, dear. Go handle your business. We'll talk more later," Lily said, waving goodbye. We headed to the car, feeling grateful for our warm welcome and excited about our new business venture in Pinecrest Falls.

We drove to City Hall, which was conveniently located just up the road from us, and parked in the lot across the street. As we approached the building, I couldn't help but notice its grandeur. The City Hall building was a massive stone structure that towered three stories high. A magnificent golden dome sat atop the building, adorned with gold eagles at each corner. The dome was so bright and shiny that it almost sparkled in the sunlight. Right beneath the dome was a massive clock with gleaming gold hands that caught the light and shone brilliantly. As we walked up the steps, I noticed that there were four pillars in front of the building that provided some much-needed shade. The glass doors leading inside the building were grand and imposing.

As we got closer, something caught my eye. To the side of the building, I saw a parking lot filled with about seven police cars. It struck me as odd since City Hall is not the usual spot for police cars to be parked. I wondered what could be going on inside the building that would warrant such a police presence. Despite my curiosity, we continued walking towards the entrance, eager to discover what secrets lay within the walls of City Hall.

As we walked through the front door of the city hall, we were greeted by a friendly and efficient-looking secretary. She had short blond hair, wore a blue shirt that complemented her eyes, and had large reading glasses perched on the tip of her nose. Judging by her appearance and demeanor, I guessed she was in her late twenties.

The secretary politely asked us which department we were looking for, to which my Mom replied that we were there to pick up her business license. The secretary graciously guided us toward the records section, which was a few doors down the hallway.

As we walked, I again noticed several police cars parked in the lot outside the building. Curious, I asked the secretary about it, and she explained that since the town was not very big, the police department had decided to house their station in the basement of the town hall to save on costs. She added that the basement had a completely different layout than the floors above, which were used by the city hall for administrative purposes.

Intrigued by the idea of visiting the police station, I asked my Mom if it was okay for me to go and check it out. I thought it would be an excellent opportunity to capture some content for my social media accounts. My Mom agreed, on the condition that I took my younger brother along with me. We parted ways with my Mom, who went upstairs to take care of her business, while we made our way towards the basement to explore the police station.

As we made our way downstairs, I couldn't help but notice how different the atmosphere was from upstairs. The lighting was dimmer, giving off a more serious and professional vibe. It was evident that we had entered the basement section of the building. We approached a pair of double wood doors that had blue lettering that read "Pinecrest Fall Police Station" and pushed them open. The room we entered was enormous, with a brown ceiling and grey carpeted floor.

As I entered the room, I was struck by the sight of eight large office desks arranged in a neat line. Each desk was unique in its own way, with personal touches that reflected the individuality of the police officers who occupied them. Some desks were adorned with pictures of loved ones, while others displayed sports memorabilia or toys. I couldn't help but notice the Pokemon toys on one desk and the Dallas Cowboys football jersey on another. It was fascinating to see how each officer had personalized their workspace.

On the other side of the room, a sturdy door with a police seal caught my attention. Beneath it, a nameplate indicated the room's purpose, with labels like "Holding" or "Interrogation." I made a conscious effort to avoid these rooms, knowing that they were used for detaining suspects and conducting questioning. I was impressed by the room's overall set-up, which appeared professional and efficient. The police department had taken great care in creating a work-space that was both functional and welcoming to its officers.

A sense of eeriness took over us as we stood in the room. We looked around and realized the place was empty. The reception desk was deserted, and none of the computers were switched on. I called out for someone, but my voice echoed back at us. We waited for what felt like an eternity, and just as we were about to leave, a door in the far corner opened. Out walked a tall man with a shiny bald head and an enormous black and grey mustache that starkly contrasted his milky white skin. His big belly was prominent, but his strong-looking arms and legs made him seem quite fit. He was wearing a bright green jacket with a badge on the arm that read "Pinecrest Fall Sheriff."

He had a warm smile on his face as he walked over to us and introduced himself. "Well, Hello there. My name is Sheriff Owen Wells, but you can call me Owen," he said cheerfully. We introduced ourselves to the Sheriff, and I told him that my name was Hazel

Torres and my brother's name was Griffin Torres. We had just moved to the town and wanted to explore the police station.

Owen seemed delighted that we wanted to come and visit, and he asked us if we wanted to be police officers one day. I told him that I wanted to be a detective, which made him even more excited. "That's exciting. We only have one detective here at the station. I bet he would love to meet you," Owen said while he pulled out chairs for us to sit.

As we settled into our seats, I looked around the empty room and asked Owen where everyone was. He explained that everyone was out doing patrols since they barely got any calls, which was typical of small-town living. Suddenly, we heard the door open, and my Mom came laughing in, followed by someone else.

As they stepped into the room, I noticed a tall white man with short black hair and a thick beard. He had lines under his eyes and looked like he had stayed up late the night before. He was wearing a grey button-down shirt, black slacks, and brown dress shoes. The man walked in with our Mom, laughing like he had just told a joke. "Oh, speaking about our detective, here he is now. I would like for you guys to meet Detective Leo Davis. Leo, this is Hazel and Griffin Torres.

Who do you have with you?" Owen asked. "Oh, this is Olivia Torres; she is their mother. I met her on the way down here. Your kids look just like you, Olivia," Leo said, smiling at my Mom. "They look more like their father than me," my Mom said, smiling at us.

"Hey, Mom, this is the Sheriff. He's super cool and was excited to hear about Hazel wanting to be a detective," my brother said, running up to them. "Wait, you want to be a detective? That's exciting. Maybe I'll have a partner in the future," Leo said. My brother couldn't contain his curiosity and started asking Leo questions: "So, Leo, how many cases have you solved? Do you go on late-night stakeouts? Do you go on car chases through the city? How many suspects have you put away?" Leo didn't seem bothered by the questions and answered them with a calm demeanor. My Mom told Griffin to stop, and everyone started laughing.

Opening my eyes, I noticed a board with five pictures of missing children on the wall. The children were young as if they had been in middle school. The posters spoke to me as if something had come over me. This feeling only came to me when I knew a new case was about to start. I walked over and looked at the most recent photo, which was from five years ago, of a little Asian girl with a red ribbon with a gold bird tied in her black hair. It looks like Griffin was right; there will always be a mystery to solve.

Chapter Two
The Investigation Begin

As I shifted my gaze back to the detective, I was filled with a sense of unease and curiosity about the case of the five missing children. Unable to resist my curiosity, I inquired about the case, hoping to glean some information about what happened to them. The detective's response was measured and cautious,

"I'm sorry, but this is an ongoing investigation, and I cannot share many details. However, I can assure you that we are doing everything in our power to find them, and we still believe that they are out there somewhere." As he spoke, the detective walked over to the wall next to me, where several posters with pictures of the missing children were hanging.

As I stood in front of the bulletin board, my eyes fixated on each poster, I couldn't help but notice the stark similarities in the children's disappearances. The first thing that stood out to me was the pattern of the years each child went missing. It was clear that each disappearance occurred every five years, spanning over a period of 25 years. The most recent missing child vanished in 2023, followed by disappearances in 2018, 2013, 2008, and 2003. The fact that there had been no resolution or closure for any of these cases left a sense of unease in the pit of my stomach.

As I stood there with Leo by my side, I couldn't help but feel a sense of unease. I turned to him and spoke in a hushed tone, "Leo, did you know that the disappearances in this town take place every five years? And, we are in the fifth year now, so a child would most likely disappear soon if one hasn't already." Leo's eyes widened in shock as he listened to my words. I could see the worry and concern written all over his face. But I didn't stop there. I continued to share what I had noticed, hoping it would help us understand the situation better.

"I've also observed that each kid who has disappeared is under the age of 13. So, if someone is kidnapping them, they would be looking for young kids around my brother's age," I said, my voice filled with concern. As I spoke those words, I couldn't help but wonder what was happening in our town. Who was behind these disappearances? And, most importantly, how could we stop them before it was too late? However, Leo did not seem to agree with my theory and said that they did not believe the kids were taken; they believed they were runaways. But that did not click with me. I asked Leo, "If they were runaways, where is the parent's contact information? The only number to call would be the police station."

Leo appeared to be taken aback by the suggestion that the missing children might have been kidnapped. He explained that the children in question were orphans and had no biological family to return to. As a result, the police force had presumed that the kids had run away from the orphanages as they didn't want to stay there any longer. Leo shared that his father, who had been the sheriff before he passed away, had been leading the case initially. However, Leo took over the investigation about seven years ago. Despite his best efforts, he couldn't find any lead on the missing children. Leo acknowledged that he had noticed a pattern in which every five years, one kid would run away and get lost. He believed that it was some kind of kid prank that went too far. Perhaps they thought it was amusing, but it had cost them their lives as they were still missing, and the possibility of them surviving was bleak.

However, Leo couldn't ignore the other possibilities that something more sinister might have happened to the children. When I suggested that the clues didn't match up with the theory of the children running away, Leo conceded that I might be right. He realized that he had been fixated on the idea of the children running away without considering the possibility of kidnapping.

As my curiosity got the best of me, I couldn't help but ask questions. I was eager to find out more about the case of the missing children. But my Mom, who was with me at the time, reminded me that we were not in New Mexico, and it wasn't appropriate to question law enforcement officers about their cases. However, Leo didn't seem to mind my inquiries and responded, "It's alright. I don't mind it at all. I guess you want to be a detective when you grow up."

"My father was the sheriff in our town and an exceptional detective. He had a knack for solving challenging cases, and he was highly respected by everyone in the community. His presence was truly integral to the town. I deeply miss him and the valuable guidance he provided. Taking over this case from him was a significant responsibility, and I made a promise to continue investigating it, even if it initially seemed straightforward. Your inquisitiveness is truly commendable. It's heartening to witness young individuals like yourself approaching their career paths with such dedication." Leo said

Just as Leo finished his sentence, the phone rang, and he had to attend to the call. However, I wasn't done with my line of questioning, as I was determined to piece together the clues and unravel the mystery of the missing children. The case had piqued my interest, and I was eager to learn more about it. I wondered what clues the police had uncovered so far and what their next move would be. Despite the interruption, my mind was still racing with thoughts and possibilities, and I couldn't wait to learn more about the case.

As my brother Griffin continued to converse with the sheriff, I couldn't help but wonder if he had any additional information about the missing children. Curious, I approached him and politely asked if he could provide any further details about the case. The sheriff, with a solemn expression, informed me that he could not discuss the case any further since it was still active. My Mom, who noticed my curiosity, pulled me aside and cautioned me to stop asking questions.

Despite the sheriff's response, Griffin was not content with the lack of information and continued to probe for more details. He questioned the sheriff about the possible whereabouts of the orphans, suggesting that they would have had nowhere to run away if they were indeed orphans. The sheriff replied that they believed the children had gone into the woods and become lost. This response perplexed Griffin, who then turned to me and asked why the authorities had not been able to find the children yet, or even a body if they had perished in the woods.

As the conversation continued between Griffin and the sheriff, it became clear that Griffin's incessant questioning had taken a toll on his mother's patience. Her frustration was palpable, and it was evident that she was getting angry. Just then,

Leo returned and spoke up, stating that they stood by their investigation and firmly believed that the children had run away and gotten lost in the woods. However, he also added that if the worst had happened, they believed that the wildlife in the area would have taken care of the bodies.

Despite Leo's words, the implication that they were withholding information and manipulating the case in their favor was obvious. It left a sour taste in the mouths of those present, including Griffin. Although Griffin was about to ask another question, I gave him a subtle look, urging him to refrain. As much as I wanted to push for the truth, I could sense that my mother was already at her limit. Sometimes, it's better to pick your battles, and this was one of those moments.

When preparing to leave, my mother expressed her gratitude to Owen and Leo for their warm hospitality and extended her hopes of seeing them again in the near future. Owen, in turn, promised to pay a visit to their shop whenever possible and bring home fresh flowers for his beloved wife. Leo, who didn't have a significant other, also pledged to pay a visit to the shop and add some color to his life. When my mother asked if Leo was married or had a girlfriend, he replied with an affirmative "No" and added that he was still searching for someone special and hadn't given up hope yet. As they exchanged their goodbyes and started walking back to the car, my brother and I couldn't help but notice a slight blush on our mother's cheeks, indicating that she was a little taken aback by Leo's comment.

As we were getting ready to leave, I made sure to grab a poster for each of the five missing children. My determination to solve this case and bring some closure to these kids, even if they were orphans, was unshakable. We had been given a daunting task, but we were all resolved to see it through to the end, no matter what obstacles we might encounter along the way. Despite our collective determination, I couldn't shake the feeling that something was amiss. There was a nagging suspicion in the pit of my stomach that told me not to trust Leo. I couldn't pinpoint exactly what made me uneasy around him, but something about his demeanor didn't sit right with me. However, I put my reservations aside and focused on the task at hand.

Chapter Three
Setting Up Shop

As we walked back to our car, I noticed my Mom still had an angry look on her face, which made me feel a little uneasy. So I decided to ask her if she was still mad at us for asking questions about the case of missing children. She stopped right in the parking lot and turned to me with a furious expression in her eyes. "We just moved here for a fresh start, and you can't help but try to find a new case to solve," she said. "I thought if we moved, you might slow down with the mystery-solving, but I guess I was wrong. And now you also have your brother involved in this. You two know better than to ask police officers about their case and then start questioning their work. Do you know how disrespectful that was?"

I tried to reason with her by saying, "But Mom, you have to agree that none of what they said was adding up. They are clearly hiding something." However, my mother was not convinced, and she sharply replied, "That is not your concern. You are not a real detective. I don't care how many cases you solved back in New Mexico, and this is not the same thing as trying to find someone's bike or a missing cat." I was feeling a bit frustrated at this point and said, "I don't see what the problem is; you've never had a problem when I question the police back home, so why is it different here?"

"It's different here because these are not our people. We did not grow up in this community. We are outsiders looking in, and you are already causing trouble," my Mom explained. I understood where she was coming from, but I couldn't turn a blind eye to 25 years of missing children, especially when they were around Griffin's age. "Oh, I understand that complete-ly, but I'm not going to turn a blind eye to 25 years of missing children, especially when they are around Griffin's age. I thought you would have taken a bigger notice of that," I rea-soned.

"Don't start getting smart with me. I did notice that, but Griffin is my son, and I'll worry about him not miss-ing kids who are not mine," my Mom retorted. Griffin, who had been qui-et until then, spoke up and said, "It looked like to me you were more wor-ried about what Leo taught than wor-rying about me." My Mom turned to him and said, "You don't know what you're talking about, and you need to watch your mouth."

Griffin looked my Mom in the eyes and said, "That guy is nowhere near the man that Dad was. I thought you would have gotten a crush on someone who was more like him." My Mom turned red, and I couldn't tell if it was from embarrassment or from rage.

"I understand what you're saying, Mom, and we're sorry. We didn't mean to upset you. But this is our thing. It's what me and Griffin shared with Dad. Solving clues and catching bad guys. Remember, Dad called us the Latino Hardy siblings," I said, hoping she would understand. Her

face went from red back to her normal color. "I see where you two are
coming from. I won't stop you two
from investigating, but no more asking police questions, and if it gets too
dangerous, then you pull back. Am I
clear?" My Mom said.

My brother and I both nodded in
agreement. "Now, let's head home
and get some food. I can't wait to
use the kitchen fully," my Mom said
cheerfully. We all loaded up in the car
and started the ride back to our new
home, feeling a bit relieved that my
Mom had finally understood our perspective.

As soon as Griffin and my Mom got home, I immediately headed to the attic to start setting up my new workplace. Unlike my old room, which only had a small corner designated for my work, the attic offered ample space for me to spread out and get organized. Having everything laid out in front of me helps me think better and work more efficiently.

After rummaging through some of the moving boxes, I found all the supplies I needed - notebooks, yellow notepads, pens, pencils, tape, and highlighters. With all my tools in hand, I laid them out neatly on the big table in the center of the room. As I was looking around, I noticed a large standing chalkboard that had been hidden away in the corner. I pulled it over to the center of the room and taped a picture of all five missing kids on it.

I then scoured the room for some chalk and eventually found it in a little box on the other side of the room. Using the chalk, I began writing everything I already knew about the missing kids in the empty space beside their picture. I wrote down all the information I had gathered so far, including the fact that all the kids who had gone missing were under 13 years old and were orphans. I also noted that the disappearances had occurred every five years.

Once I had written down everything I knew, I sat down in one of the wooden chairs and took the time to study each of the missing kids' pictures on the wall. I felt determined to find out what had happened to them and was ready to start my investigation.

Let's take a closer look at each kid's picture. First up is Tommy, a freckle-faced boy with untamed brown hair and a playful grin that exudes mischief. Next on the list is Emily, a dainty girl with curly blonde locks that frame her bright blue eyes, giving her a delicate and angelic appearance. Following her is Carlos, a young boy with deep black hair and olive skin, his eyes brimming with curiosity and wonder. Then there is Sophia, a somewhat tall young girl with long dark tresses that cascade down her back, her piercing gaze exuding a sense of determination. Last but not least, we have Linh, an Asian girl with short black hair and sparkling brown eyes that reflect her youthful spirit. She dons a bright red ribbon in her hair, embellished with the symbol of a gold eagle, a testament to her courage and resilience. Despite their differences, each of these kids shares one thing in common that they were all orphans.

As I sat in the dimly lit room, I couldn't help but feel overwhelmed. I had been trying to decipher why certain individuals were singled out from a group, but I couldn't seem to find any commonality among them. The frustration was starting to set in. Just then, my brother Griffin walked in and complimented my workspace. He pulled up a chair and asked about my progress. I sighed and told him that I had hit a dead end. I had already gone through all the information I had and still couldn't find anything that tied them together.

Griffin suggested that we should look at which orphanage the kids had lived in. It was a brilliant idea that hadn't occurred to me. I quickly took out my iPhone and searched for any orphanages in Pinecrest Falls. Fortunately, there was only one, "Hope's Reuge." I scribbled the name on the chalkboard, and we both leaned back to survey our work. The name stood out, and I couldn't help but feel a sense of relief wash over me. Maybe we were finally getting somewhere.

As we were engrossed in our conversation, we suddenly heard our Mom's voice calling out to us that dinner was ready. We both jumped up, grateful for the interruption, as our stomachs had started to grumble. "Let's put a pin in this and go get some food. I might be able to think better on a full stomach," I said as I made my way towards the door. Griffin nodded in agreement, "Yeah,

I agree. I can't think straight being this hungry." As we started to walk down the stairs, I turned to look at my brother, who seemed lost in thought. I asked him what was on his mind. He looked at me and said, "Well, I was thinking, if this has been going on for 25 years, then someone other than Leo must have worked on this case. He was only in his thirties or mid-thirties, right? He couldn't have been the only cop to investigate this." I nodded my head in agreement, knowing that it was a valid point. However, we had no way of finding out since we couldn't question the police again. "Let's head downstairs before Mom comes and gets us," I said, trying to change the topic. We both made our way down, eager to eat and recharge ourselves after a long day. Despite our hunger, we couldn't help but feel that we had made some progress in our investigation.

As we descended the stairs, the aroma of Mom's culinary creations wafted up to our nostrils. The dining table was a sight to behold, adorned with a plethora of our favorite dishes. The tacos were brimming with succulent grilled steak, topped with a generous helping of cheese, lettuce, and juicy tomatoes. The paella was a masterpiece, the rice steaming with delectable chunks of steak and veggies. The freshly baked empanadas were irresistible, their tantalizing scent betraying the savory chicken inside. The golden arepas were complemented perfectly by a side of ripe, velvety avocados. And last but not least, the ceviche - my absolute favorite. Its tangy, zesty flavor was perfectly balanced with the fresh seafood, leaving my taste buds tingling with delight.

As we sat at the dinner table, enjoying the delicious food that my Mom had ordered from Uber Eats, I couldn't help but ask where all this food came from. My mom explained that she had the groceries delivered while we were upstairs. Meanwhile, my brother Griffin was busy stuffing his face with empanadas and washing them down with lemonade. Finally, he stopped to catch his breath and exclaimed, "Mom, we haven't had food this good in such a long time. I missed it so much. No more fast food burgers for me!" I chuckled and took another bite of my ceviche.

Just as I was about to ask my Mom about the case of the missing kids, she put her hand up and said, "Not at the dinner table, you both can save that for the attic. But we do need to talk about the shop." She pushed aside one of the tacos and continued, "I want to get the shop open by the end of next week. I don't think it would be smart to wait too long because there is already a buzz around town, and we don't want to lose that. I'm going to need both of your help with this, and it won't be easy. Do you two think you can help?"

My brother and I exchanged a knowing look and a wink, and we both eagerly agreed to help our Mom with the flower shop. She looked visibly relieved and continued, "Tomorrow, we will head back to the shop and get everything cleaned up. I will order the signs, flowers, and all the media promotions that we will need. I also want to get some pottery from Lily so we can sell them as packages.

I need you kids to get the front and back of the shop ready, throw away anything we don't need, and set up the front in a way that everyone can see what we've got."

Excitement filled the air as my brother and I nodded our heads in agreement. I couldn't help but ask, "Did you come up with a name for the shop yet?" A big grin spread across my Mom's face as she replied, "Yes, I named the shop 'Flowers by Torres.' What do you guys think?" My brother and I jumped out of our seats, telling our Mom how much we loved the name. She clapped with excitement and reminded us to finish our food because we were going to need the energy for tomorrow.

As soon as we finished our meal and cleaned up the dishes, I made my way back to my room. I needed to review my notes one more time before going to bed, so I retrieved my notebook from the attic. Despite feeling quite drained after a long day, I was excited about the prospect of helping my mother achieve her dream of owning a flower shop. However, I couldn't shake off the thought of the five missing children. Although I was aware that I couldn't ask the police any more questions, I knew there was more to the case than what they were letting on. Detective Leo had been particularly evasive, and I was convinced that he was hiding something. Those children had been taken, and just because they were orphans didn't mean their lives were any less valuable than anyone else's. I was determined to uncover the truth and put this 25-year-old mystery to rest.

I walked over to the desk in my room and carefully positioned it so that I could have my back to the curtain. As I did this, I grabbed my phone and set it up on the sturdy tripod that my Dad had given me for Christmas. I was feeling a bit nervous and excited because I wanted to start a livestream, but at the same time, I didn't want strangers to see my room. So, I always made sure the curtain was my background. I learned this trick from a friend who was an experienced live streamer.

To ensure my privacy and safety, I also made sure I never wore any makeup or revealing clothing during my livestreams. You never know who is watching, and I didn't want to attract any unwanted attention. I recently found out that I could do a livestream on Facebook and Instagram at the same time. This was a huge relief for me because I'm not the best at working with technology, and it made things a lot easier for me.

Now, I could reach out to my audience on both platforms without any extra effort.

After starting the stream, I took the time to introduce myself to my followers, who have been eagerly waiting for updates from me. I was apologetic for not posting in a while, but I had a good reason for it - I had moved to a new state. Most of my followers are familiar with me from my previous life in New Mexico, where they started following me because I would take them along with me when I was working on a case. Now, my family and I are fully settled in our new home, and I am excited to share some news with everyone.

My new partner on this case is my brother, who stumbled upon our new case in the town where we are currently living. Five children, all under the age of 13, have gone missing, and the police are trying to say that the children ran away. However, I don't believe that for a second. The craziest part is that the children were taken every five years, and all of them were orphans. It's shocking that after 25 years of children going missing, people still turn a blind eye to it.

As an investigator, I have a theory that the children were taken every five years before they turned into teenagers. The police here want us to believe that the children ran away, but the clues don't suggest that. My brother and I are both on the case, and we are determined to solve it faster than the cops. Rest assured that we will do everything possible to uncover the truth and bring justice to the families affected by this tragedy.

As I ended the live stream, I could see a stream of heart emojis and likes flying up the screen. Many of my followers were cheering me on, urging me to find the missing kids. "You're the only one who can do it," read one of the comments, filled with encouragement and hope. However, there were also a few negative comments that I chose to ignore. Since I didn't know those people personally, their comments didn't affect me much. Af-ter all, I had shared my story with my followers, hoping that they might be of some help in my search.

As I said my goodbyes to my audi-ence, I felt a sense of relief wash over me. The stream had been emotional-ly draining, and I was ready to un-wind. I rested my head on the softest pillow I had ever felt and listened to the peaceful silence surrounding me. The wind was whistling outside, but the sound was soothing and serene. It was a perfect evening, and I had no trouble falling asleep.

As I slowly regained consciousness in the morning, my phone alarm went off, making me jump a little. I rubbed my eyes and sat up, feeling a little dizzy from the sudden wake-up call. Despite this, I got up anyway, determined to start the day off right. I made my way to the bathroom, where I took a refreshing shower and got myself ready for the busy day ahead. Today, we were all going out to the flower shop to get everything cleaned up, which was sure to be a long and tiring task. I needed an outfit that would be both functional and comfortable, so I opted for some overalls and old shoes that I'd never really worn before. To keep my hair out of the way, I found a green bandana that I could tie up in a neat little knot.

As I made my way downstairs, I saw my Mom sitting on the couch in the living room, talking on the phone. She was wearing a bright yellow polo shirt and some work jeans, and she looked up at me as I walked past, giving me a small smile. I didn't want to disturb her conversation, so I just gave her a nod and kept walking towards the kitchen.

Once in the kitchen, I was greeted by the delicious aroma of pancakes. My brother Griffin was sitting at the table, happily munching away on his breakfast. He looked up and saw me, offering me some pancakes. I couldn't resist, so I sat down across from him and grabbed a plate, piling it high with fluffy, golden pancakes. I poured some syrup over them, relishing in the rich, sweet flavor.

I couldn't help but marvel at how these pancakes tasted so much better than usual. "When did Mom learn how to make pancakes like this?" I asked Griffin, my mouth full of food. "I asked her too, and she said she just followed a YouTube video on how to make them perfect." He replied, still eating away. "Well, I hope she keeps making them like this," I said, taking another bite.

As Griffin and I sat at the kitchen table finishing up our pancakes, our

Mom walked in with a warm smile and asked us if we liked them. We both nodded enthusiastically, and she looked pleased. After thanking her, she informed us that we needed to hurry because she was going to have a busy day on the phone, and we had to do some shopping. We quickly stood up and put our dishes away, feeling excited about getting the flower shop ready.

As we sat in the car, she explained her plan for the day. She was going to phone numerous flower vendors to get a better understanding of how they operate. She knew it was going to be tiresome because dealing with flower vendors can be tricky, especially when it comes to pricing and delivery. However, she was determined to stick to her budget.

Curious, I asked her how many vendors she was planning to call. She replied that there were 15 different flower farms in the area, and each of them had the flowers we needed. However, depending on the farm's price, we might have to purchase two types of flowers from one farm and another four types of flowers from another. I could understand her concern. We wanted to be fair to the vendors, but we also had a bottom line that we had to adhere to. The detective world is tough, but the business world can be even tougher. Nonetheless, my Mom was steadfast in her approach and was determined to get the best deal possible.

As we finally made it to the shop, both my brother and I were eager to start cleaning and making it our own. My Mom headed directly to the backroom to make some important phone calls while I grabbed some trash cans and started to throw the junk left behind by the previous owner. We decided to keep the paper on the windows to avoid any unwanted attention until the shop was ready. It was strange to think about how people were probably passing by the window, and we could hear the crowds marching by, but we couldn't see them.

We worked together to make two piles of the items we found. The first pile contained things we knew we wouldn't need, while the second pile contained things we could possibly reuse. To make things more fun, Griffin and I decided to turn the cleaning process into a game. We both started collecting the trash, and the person who collected the most would win.

As we kept going, I noticed that I was losing for sure. Everything I found was something that we could use, like display stands, a chalkboard sign, and old baskets that could hold flowers. On the other hand, Griffin only found junk and old plants that had dried out and left an unpleasant odor. It became clear that the previous owner of the shop was maybe a herbalist or something, as I kept finding little net bags filled with old herbs and little bottles of tinctures. The shop had an overall feeling of being made to display plants, and we could see why.

After four hours of hard work, the shop looked completely different. We rearranged everything to meet our needs, and the shelves were clear, the tables were wiped clean, and the old baskets were placed in a position that would let the bouquet of flowers display nicely in front of the large window. All we needed now were some beautiful flowers to complete the look.

My Mom emerged from the back of the shop, holding her notepad in one hand and her phone in the other. She had a big smile on her face, and I could tell that she had good news to share. "I got everything that we were looking for, and it looks like we will only need to work with five different vendors," she said as she walked towards us. I immediately took a seat on one of the chairs, eager to hear more about the flowers we would be getting. My brother followed suit and sat on the other chair. My Mom sat on the table and flipped over her notepad.

She listed out all the flowers she had managed to get - roses, peonies, lilies, sunflowers, gladiolus, Zinnias, cosmos, and snapdragons.

But one flower was missing from the list—dahlias. My Mom looked a bit disappointed as she told us that none of the vendors seemed to have them. "I really wanted to find some, but none of the vendors grow any, and they didn't want to tell me who might have some. But I'll keep looking because someone has to have some," she said, determined to find the elusive flower.

A soft knock on the door caught our attention, and my Mom invited the person to come in. The door creaked open, and we saw our neighbor, Evelyn, holding a plate of delicious lemon squares. She greeted us warmly and asked how we were doing. Griffin and I simultaneously replied that we were doing well and would love to have a lemon square. Evelyn placed the plate on the table in the center of our shop, and we all gathered around to savor the delectable treats. The lemon squares were divine, with a perfect balance of sweetness and tanginess. It was clear that Evelyn was a talented baker.

After we finished the lemon squares, my Mom asked Evelyn what had brought her over. Evelyn mentioned that she had heard some noise next door and assumed we were cleaning the shop. She had informed her customers that a new flower shop would be opening soon, and they all seemed excited about it. Evelyn also wanted to check up on us and offer any assistance we might need.

My Mom explained that we had already lined up all the flower vendors but were having trouble tracking down someone who had dahlias. Evelyn had a solution to our problem and suggested calling Wolfkin's Flowers. She told us that Wolfkin's Flowers was the only farm in the area that grew dahlias because Wolfkin's dahlias were better than everyone else's. Other farmers had tried to compete with her, but no one could match the quality of her dahlias. Evelyn warned us that Wolfkin was old school and might not have a website. She suggested checking the phone book for her number.

My Mom was thankful for Evelyn's suggestion and wanted to contact Wolfkin right away. Evelyn informed her that the owner's name was Lara Wolfkin, and my Mom went to the back of the shop to search for an old phone book. With Evelyn's assistance, we were now one step closer to finding the ideal dahlias for our store.

During a conversation with Evelyn, she asked me how my brother and I were adjusting. I replied, "To be honest, we haven't had a chance to fully settle in yet. We've been focused on getting the shop ready to open. However, we have enjoyed our time here so far, and we've been struck by how kind and friendly everyone is."

While I was speaking, Griffin was still busy eating, but he enthusiastically chimed in, "The food here is absolutely delicious! You're an amazing baker. Where did you learn how to do this?" Evelyn beamed with pride and began sharing a story about her mother, who had started the bakery when Evelyn was just a little girl. She would watch her mother bake all day on the weekends, and when she came home from school, she would go to the bakery and watch her Mom bake for hours into the night.

Evelyn went on to explain how, as she got older, she started working for her mother and eventually took over the business after her Mom retired. Listening to her talk about her Mom, I couldn't help but think about how much my brother and I care for our own mother. Evelyn's joy and pride in her family business were truly heart-warming.

Mom finally emerged from the back and announced, "I managed to get in touch with her, and she wants us to come visit the farm tomorrow to see the place. Evelyn, you were right. She prefers to do business in person rather than over the phone." Evelyn stood up and said, "I've met her a few times, and that's definitely like her. I hope you all enjoy the trip. I need to get back to the bakery before I lose too many customers. Let me know if you need anything." We all said goodbye as she walked out the door. I turned to my Mom and asked, "So, where are we going?" My Mom replied, "To-morrow morning, we're heading to Emerald Valley. Now, let's pack up and head home. I think we've done enough for today."

It was getting late, and I found my-self back in the attic, poring over my notes. Although I was keen to dig around for more information, I was pressed for time as my priority was my mother's flower shop. The missing children were also of great concern to me, but my mother's business needed to be successful. Suddenly, my brother Griffin entered the room and asked what I was doing. I replied, "I'm getting my notes together before starting my livestream. Do you want to join me?" He nodded excitedly, as he had never been in one of my live streams before. "I'm going to set up my phone on the tripod and start the stream. We'll introduce ourselves and explain what we have so far. We'll use the chalkboard as our backdrop and show the picture of the missing kids. If you feel uncomfortable at any moment, just walk out of the frame, okay?" I reassured him, and he gave me a thumbs up. He took a few deep breaths and stood beside the chalkboard. I set up the tripod, positioned my phone, and began the livestream.

"Good evening, everyone. I hope you're all doing well. I know it's late, but I thought it was crucial to share some more information with you regarding the case we're working on. For those of you who don't know me, my name is Hazel Torres, and I'd like to introduce you to my partner in this case, my brother Griffin Torres. He's been a great support to me, and we'll be working together to solve this mystery." As Griffin waves hello, I notice a flurry of hearts and likes appearing on my phone screen. A few comments follow, praising how cute and adorable my brother is. I can see Griffin's cheeks turning red with shyness, but I continue with the briefing.

"Behind us, you can see the pictures of the five children we're investigating. Their names are Tommy Schmidt, Emily Wanger, Carlos Santos, Sophia Khan, and Linh Li. We believe that these children have been abducted, but the police are hiding this information and going with the story that the children ran away. What we know so far is that each child was an orphan and that all of them were under the age of thirteen." Griffin interjects, adding that the kidnappings took place five years apart, and since this year marks the fifth year, we fear that another child will go missing if we don't act fast. I smile and nod, grateful for his input.

"We plan to investigate the orphanage where the children were housed next. We're looking for a pattern to see what the kidnappers are looking for, besides the children's age. We hope to have more information to share with you next time we talk. But for now, we need to get some rest and prepare for tomorrow." With that, I turn off the stream, thanking everyone for tuning in and promising to update them as we learn more.

"That was fun," Griffin said. "I'm glad you liked it. Next time, I'll have you speak more. But for now, let's head to bed. We have a flower farm to visit in the morning," I replied. We packed everything up and headed towards the door. Griffin walked down the steps first, and before I left, I looked back at the missing poster of the children, thinking in my head that we are going to solve this and bring closure for those kids.I turned off the lights and went to bed to get a good night's sleep for tomorrow.

Chapter Four
Crafting a Plan

Later that afternoon, Griffin and I found ourselves back in the attic, surrounded by our notes and newspaper clippings. We pored over our findings, trying to connect the dots and make sense of the puzzle we had stumbled upon. It became clear to us that Leo and his father had been involved in concealing the children's disappearances, carefully hiding the truth from the community. We uncovered how they had been selecting their victims, but a recent change in leadership had disrupted their sinister operation.

As I reflected on what Ileana had confided in me, recounting the chilling sounds of children's cries emanating from the basement alongside billowing black smoke from the chimney every five years, a shiver ran down my spine. The timing of these occurrences aligned with the years of the children's disappearances, revealing a haunting pattern. However, the pièce de résistance was the discovery of a red ribbon adorned with a golden eagle, discarded on the dusty basement floor. It was a serendipitous find, a missing link that brought clarity to our investigation.

I couldn't help but ponder the unlikely sequence of events that had led us here. If I hadn't chanced upon the room where the ladies were playing music and met Ileana, we might have never received this crucial lead. It felt like a stroke of fortune, a fortuitous turn of events that we needed to make the most of. Whether it was divine intervention or sheer luck, we were determined to seize this unexpected blessing and pursue the truth with unwavering resolve.

"What do you think Lara was doing down in the basement with those kids?" Griffin asked, his brow fur-rowed with concern. I paused, con-templating his question as I glanced up at the ceiling. It was a valid point - we were left with more questions than answers. The only tangible evi-dence we had was the red ribbon, a haunting reminder of the children's presence. "I honestly don't know," I admitted, feeling a sense of unease settle over me. "But we do know Linh was down there. We need concrete in-formation. Relying solely on a video of a red ribbon in a basement is ten-uous at best. Lara could easily claim it as her own." I shook my head, the weight of the situation heavy on my shoulders. "And I don't want to involve Ileana and her sisters. It could do more harm than good." Standing up, I walked over to the window, seeking solace in the swaying tree leaves outside. "We also have no knowledge of how Leo managed to bring Linh to the basement or what his connection to Lara Wolfkin is. Are they working together? Was he selling the children to her? There are too many unknowns," Griffin mused, his voice tinged with frustration.

He was right. Despite our best efforts, we still couldn't figure out the connection or motive behind Leo and Lara's actions. Why did they need the kids? Why did they only strike every five years? And why were they exclusively targeting orphans? Moreover, the mystery of the chimney emitting black smoke on a five-year cycle added another layer of perplexity. Even with all the pieces laid out in front of us, I couldn't shake the feeling that there were more puzzle pieces we hadn't uncovered. As I gazed out the window, pondering our next course of action, only one risky plan came to mind. It was so perilous that I hesitated to voice it aloud. Yet, if we were to bring this enigma to a close, it seemed like the only viable option.

I glanced over at Griffin and took a deep breath as I gazed down at the attic floor. "I need to get into that basement," I stated. Griffin stood up and asked if I was out of my mind. Trying to hold back tears, I looked at Griffin, wondering if my plan was too dangerous to ask my brother to participate in. "Griffin, I have a plan to get into the basement, but I need your help. It puts you in more danger than me, so I really don't want to do this." Tears were streaming down my face, and I could barely get my words out. This was crazy; there was no way we could go through with this. What kind of sister was I? Griffin walked over to me and hugged me. "We are in this together, Hazel. You and me, partners, right? I can handle whatever you ask me to do, and we will find justice for those kids, I promise," he said. I wiped my eyes and hugged him back. "You know, a detective should not make promises," I said. Griffin let go and looked into my eyes, saying, "Yeah, promises they can't keep."

"Alright, so here's the plan. I need to access the basement, but it's not going to be a walk in the park. I'll have to get my hands on Dad's bolt cutters and sneak them in to break the lock," I explained. "But why not just pick the lock?" Griffin inquired. "I don't know how to do that," I replied. "After we've got what we need, we're going straight to the police. It won't matter if Lara notices the lock is gone. While I'm doing that, I need you to keep Lara occupied. I'm uneasy about you being alone with her, but I need you to divert her attention from me. I'll make an excuse to take a phone call and step away. When I do, ask her to take you on another tour through the rose field. The roses are right next to the farm store, so people will be around if anything happens," I instructed.

"Alright, but how do we get back to Wolfkin Farm? They won't let us in without an appointment," Griffin questioned. "This plan won't kick off until dinner tonight," I disclosed. "What do you mean?" Griffin probed. "At dinner, I'm going to tell Mom that we need more flowers and suggest that she call Lara to place another order for pickup tomorrow," I revealed.

"Do you really think Mom will buy that?" Griffin doubted. "It'll work because Mom wants the opening to be grand, and the more flowers, the better. We've got a plan, and we just need to stick to it," I reassured. Griffin agreed that the plan sounded solid and said he would keep a low profile at dinner in case Mom was still upset with him. We've got a plan, and it's about to go into action in about an hour. Let's see if we're as good as we believe we are.

Mom's voice echoed through the house, calling us downstairs for dinner. Griffin and I made our way down from the attic to the dining room and

took our seats at the table. The entic-
ing aroma of pasta wafted from the
kitchen as my Mom emerged with a
large bowl of steaming pasta. She followed it up with a pot of rich, deep
red tomato sauce. It was pasta night,
and the sight and smell of the food
made me realize just how hungry I
was, causing my stomach to audibly
growl.

Griffin eagerly piled a generous
portion of pasta onto his plate and
doused it with the savory sauce.
Meanwhile, my Mom and I served
ourselves and began eating in con-
tented silence. After a few moments,
my Mom broke the quietude by asking about our trip to the farm. I as-

sured her that it went well and mentioned that the flowers were safely stored in the cooler at the shop. A smile graced her lips as we continued to eat.

With the evening progressing, I knew it was time to broach the topic that had been on my mind. I suggested to my Mom that we should order more flowers for the shop. Initially, she expressed confidence in our current stock for the grand opening, but I argued that having an abundance of flowers, especially unique ones like dahlias, would be beneficial since we are the only flower shop in town. After a moment of contemplation, she agreed, acknowledging the wisdom in my suggestion.

Excited about the prospect, my Mom mentioned placing an order for the following day but expressed the need for someone to pick up the flowers, as she would be tied up at the shop awaiting additional supplies. I promptly volunteered Griffin and myself for the task, assuring her that we could handle it. As my Mom left the table to make the call, the plan was starting to take shape.

"Wow, I can't believe that worked," Griffin exclaimed, his eyes wide with amazement. "It's not done yet; if Mom can't place that order, then we will have to wait another day or two.

I would really like to get this over with," I said with a tinge of frustration. Griffin paused to take another bite of his pasta before leaning in and asking, "What exactly are you going to be looking for down in the basement?" I took a moment to savor the delicious food before responding, "I'm going to search for evidence of the kids being down there. We know Linh's ribbon was found, but I'm hoping to find other pieces of clothing or something else that can confirm the kids' presence." Griffin nodded thoughtfully, showing his understanding of the importance of the task. "Are you planning to take pictures or do another video down there? You can't risk tampering with evidence," he reminded me, demonstrating his recent interest in detective vocabulary from the Sherlock Holmes books he'd been reading. "I've thought about that," I replied. "I've decided that I'm going to do another livestream down in the basement." Griffin furrowed his brow, a look of concern crossing his face. "Do you really think it's the right time to be sharing this with your followers?" he asked, clearly worried about the implications. I paused, realizing the validity of his point. Why involve social media when I should be solely focused on finding clues?

"I know it might sound a bit unconventional, but I have a specific rationale for this plan. I want to conduct a live stream to attract more attention to the basement. Since I'll be short on time, I believe that having as many people as possible tuning in could be beneficial. While I might overlook something, the viewers might notice something in a corner or on a shelf that I missed. I understand that it's not ideal to rely on strangers for help, but their input could be valuable," I explained.

"Oh, I understand your reasoning now. I think it's actually a good idea. But what if Leo sees your live stream and figures out what you're up to?" Griffin inquired. "I considered that possibility after realizing how involved Leo was in all of this. So, I took proactive steps and blocked Leo from accessing my accounts on Facebook, Instagram, and Twitter. Even if I go live, he won't be able to see what we're up to," I reassured. "Wow, Hazel, you really have thought of everything," Griffin remarked.

When Mom returned to the room and settled into her seat, she shared, "I managed to reach Lara, and she confirmed that the flowers will be ready at noon tomorrow. I informed her that it would be the two of you picking them up, and she assured me that she would inform the gate to expect you. There will be five buckets of dahlias waiting for you upon your arrival." I assured her that we would ensure the safe delivery of the flowers to the shop and express our gratitude to Lara Wolfkin for accommodating our last-minute order.

"It's been quite a challenge since we moved from New Mexico, trying to adapt to our new home and rushing to open the flower shop. I realize I've asked a lot from both of you, and I'm sorry. I want you to know that I'm doing all of this for our family. I hope that Washington will offer us a safer environment with fewer crimes, allowing us to finally settle in as a family," my Mom expressed. Griffin and

I reassured her that we understood and that we actually enjoyed living in Pinecrest, where we had already made some new friends. "Yeah, Hazel even has a new boyfriend named Miles. He lives right across the street," Griffin blurted out. I shot him a disapproving look, and he immediately became smaller in his seat. "You have a boyfriend and didn't tell me?" my Mom asked. "No, he's just a friend. We met him and his siblings, Lucas and Ava when we first moved in," I explained. My Mom smiled warmly and said, "Well, I hope to meet all of them soon."

After we finished our family dinner, we all chipped in to clean the dishes and prepare for bedtime. As everyone else settled in for the night, I retreated to my room, feeling a mix of nervousness and determination. I found myself lying on the floor, back against the wall, as I eagerly crafted posts for my social media accounts. I detailed my plans for a livestream the following day, urging my followers to tune in. The success of my elaborate plan hinged on this crucial step.

With Phase one completed—convincing our Mom to place another flower order—my mind raced through the upcoming phases. Griffin needed to keep Lara Wolfkin occupied while I snuck into the basement, the next step in our covert operation. The stakes were high as I plotted Phase three: conducting a live stream and discreetly investigating the basement for any evidence of Lara's involvement in the disappearance of the local children. The weight of our mission pressed down on me, but we had no choice but to proceed.

After ensuring my phone was charging, I carefully positioned it on the nightstand. With a sense of determination, I finally crawled into bed, my mind still swirling with the risks and possibilities ahead. As I lay my head on the pillow, I drifted off to sleep, knowing that the next day would bring both danger and the potential to finally solve the case.

Griffin and I set out the next day to Wolfkin Farm with the intention of picking up the additional dahlias my Mom had ordered. We dropped her off at the flower shop to complete some last-minute tasks before heading to the farm. However, despite assuring her that we would solely be retrieving her order, we had ulterior motives. As we made our way to the farm, Griffin and I reviewed our plan once more. His role was to keep Lara occupied by requesting another tour of the farm's rose field, which is conveniently located next to the farm store and usually bustling with people. While they were occupied, I planned to excuse myself, pretending to take a call from a college I had applied to and sneak into the basement to search for any potential clues. I was carrying my large tote bag, concealing my dad's bolt cutters, as I ventured into the basement. It was a risky endeavor, but I felt compelled to explore the basement. The success of our whole operation hinged on finding something down there. If we uncovered any evidence, our plan was to head straight to the authorities in Northcross, as we doubted the reliability of the Pinecrest police. However, if the basement yielded nothing, we would have to face the repercussions of our actions. Everything depended on my finding something down there, although I wasn't entirely sure what I was searching for. Despite the uncertainty, we were too far deep in this mission to turn back now.

I pulled our car up to the imposing iron gate and pressed the buzzer to alert the attendant of our arrival to pick up an order for Olivia Torres. The attendant acknowledged our presence and kindly opened the gate for us. I carefully maneuvered the car to the same parking spot we had used the day before. As I parked and popped the trunk, several workers emerged from the head house building with five striking buckets filled with beautiful red, white, and pink dahlias. They efficiently loaded the buckets into our car before discreetly retreating back into the building. Aware of Lara's spontaneous nature, we patiently waited, and true to form, she appeared seemingly out of nowhere, waving at us as she strolled over. After exchanging greetings, we expressed our sincere gratitude for her assistance. Lara, always gracious, assured us that it was no trouble at all and wished us great success for the flower shop's grand opening. Catching my eye, Griffin subtly signaled our pre-arranged plan. Seizing the opportunity, he smoothly requested another tour of the roses, expressing his captivation with their beauty and

fragrance. Lara readily agreed, leading us toward the rose field. Just before leaving the car, I discreetly set
an alarm on my phone to ring in
10 minutes, perfecting our planned
ruse. Seizing the moment, I fabri-
cated a call, informing Lara that it
was a long-awaited response from
a college. Politely excusing myself, I
watched as Lara and Griffin proceeded toward the rose field.

I quickly glanced around to ensure
that no one was watching as I hurried over to the old, weathered wood-
en doors leading to the basement
concealed behind the main house.
With a sense of urgency, I reached
into my bag and carefully retrieved

the heavy bolt cutters, making sure to conceal them from view. A moment of hesitation passed as I double-checked for any prying eyes before swiftly maneuvering the cutters to snap the padlock. I discreetly discarded the broken lock, ensuring it was well-hidden from sight, and cautiously swung the creaking door open before slipping into the basement.

As I made my way across the hushed basement with its white dirt floor, the soft light streaming in from the window illuminated the space. My eyes fell on the imposing furnace with its massive iron door, which seemed to serve as the base for the chimney. Shelves were stocked with charcoal and wood, neatly arranged around the furnace.

Turning to the other side of the basement, I noticed rows of shelves lined with various bags, each with different labels. One bag in particular caught my attention—it had a green tag that read "Osmocote." As I reached for it, the contents crumbled into tiny rocks in my hand. Nearby, unmarked burlap sacks piqued my curiosity. Upon opening one, I found it filled with grey ash, presumably more fertilizer.

Along the wall, white paper bags labeled "Lara's special fertilizer mix" adorned the final few shelves. I assumed these were the homemade fertilizers Lara had mentioned. Engrossed in my surroundings, I paused momentarily to retrieve my phone and prepare for the live stream.

Deciding the best vantage point would be by the basement window, I positioned my phone and set it to the wide lens to capture the entire basement as I explored. Starting the stream, I was astonished to find 200 eager viewers already waiting and joining in. "Hello, everyone, and thank you for joining me today. I need your help," I began. "The case I've been working on has gained some traction, and I require as many eyes as possible for this next phase of the investigation. I'm currently in the basement, where the five missing kids may have ended up, but I need to find proof that they were here. I'll be scouring the area, and if you spot something I might have missed, please write it in the comments. Wish me luck, everyone." As I spoke, a flurry of hearts lit up my phone screen, accompanied by a deluge of messages urging caution and safety.

I instantly launched into action, determined to find any trace that could lead me to the missing children. Scanning every inch of the room, my eyes carefully examined the surroundings, hoping to catch a glimpse of a clue that could potentially unravel this mysterious disappearance. Suddenly, as I pressed further against the back wall, my gaze fixated on something partially hidden beneath a layer of dirt. It was the same red ribbon I saw yesterday that belonged to Linh.

As I stooped down to retrieve the ribbon, my attention was drawn to a peculiar irregularity in the bricks lining the wall. Seizing the moment, I gingerly removed the loose bricks, revealing a concealed wooden chest nestled within. The anticipation kept my heart racing as I prised open the chest, ensuring my phone was capturing every moment, allowing my audience to follow this unexpected development. Inside, an unexpected

sight met my eyes – children's clothing carefully arranged within.

With a mix of curiosity and apprehension, I gingerly laid the clothes on
the floor, each piece seemingly holding a piece of the puzzle. It became
apparent that there were five sets of
clothes, each designated for a boy or
a girl. As I inspected the t-shirt, a
thought struck me – in an environment like an orphanage, ownership
is everything. The notion that each
item would bear a child's name lin-
gered in my mind, and upon inspect-
ing the neck collar, I discovered a
name meticulously inscribed on the
shirt tag. "Tommy," I voiced aloud,

ensuring my viewers were privy to this crucial discovery.

Eagerly, I continued this process, each garment unveiling a child's identity - Carlos, Sophia, Linh, and Emily. A profound sense of relief flooded over me as the pieces of this distressing puzzle came together, and the ordeal of uncertainty began to dissipate. Triumphantly, I realized that our strategy had succeeded, and the risk undertaken was not for nothing.

As I took a moment to compose myself, I carefully folded the clothes and placed them back into the wooden chest. I then pushed the chest back against the wall, making sure it was concealed from plain sight. With determination, I meticulously slid the loose bricks back into position, effectively covering any trace of my presence in the hidden room. Standing up, I felt a sense of satisfaction at successfully concealing the area. My next priority was to reunite with Griffin and leave this place. We needed to make our way to Northcross to present our findings to the authorities and bring this perplexing case to rest. However, as I brushed the dirt off my pants, I was startled by a voice behind me.

"Well, aren't you a clever girl?" I spun around in astonishment to find Leo leaning against the door, a sly grin playing on his lips.

Chapter Five
Emerald Valley

As I slowly opened my eyes, I realized that it was a long night, but at least I got some rest. My eyelids felt heavy, and my limbs even heavier. I had a long day ahead of me and knew I needed to push through the fatigue. I peeled myself out of bed, stretched my arms and legs, and headed straight for the shower. The warm water hit me in the face, helping me to fully wake up. As I stood there, I thought more about the missing child and the one puzzle piece I needed to keep the case moving. What could possibly tie all of these together to be targeted? I wish I could talk to the police more, but I knew it could put my Mom in a fury, and I didn't want to risk that. Especially if I ruined whatever she is going on with Detective Leo. That guy was obviously hiding something and got the whole town fooled. I wonder how many cases he has solved to earn so much goodwill for the sheriff to trust his judgment or if he had dirt on the sheriff, and they were both in on it together. Whatever it was, they left out some key information. I think whenever I have some free time, I'll look into Leo's background. Something from his past might shine some light on what is happening. However, I need to be careful because it would be very reckless to accuse a cop of wrongdoing. Not that it hasn't happened before, but I just moved here, and no one knows who I am. Without solid proof, I will be shut out of town.

Right now, my main focus should be the kids. If I can get to the orphanage, I could speak with someone in charge and maybe find a puzzle piece that can move us to the next step. If I can find what is the pattern between the five children, then I can see what the kidnapper was looking for. I need to figure out what the kidnapper's motive is. Were the children chosen at random, or is there something more sinister at play? It's imperative that I find answers soon. The longer we wait, the more at risk the children become. But as of now, all I have are more questions than answers. I need to stay focused and alert if I am to solve this mystery.

As I stepped out of the shower, I realized that we were going to visit a flower farm and decided to wear something comfortable. I didn't want to come off as overdressed, so I ruled out overalls. However, I still wanted to look presentable as my Mom was trying to impress a potential vendor, Lara Wolfkin, who was the only farmer in the area growing dahlias. I was curious to know what made her dahlias so unique that no one else was attempting to grow them. Maybe she had some secret techniques up her sleeve.

After brushing my hair, I went to my wardrobe to pick out an outfit. I decided to go with some thrift store clothes that I wouldn't mind getting dirty. After some contemplation, I settled for my green button-down shirt and relaxed blue jeans. I paired it with my old work boots, which I wore whenever I visited my Dad at his worksite. As I got dressed, I wondered what everyone else was going to wear. My Mom would undoubtedly wear something professional, and my brother would probably go for something basic with a cartoon character on it. But I would find out soon enough.

After finishing my hair and tying it up in a nice bun, I looked at myself in the mirror. My black and red headband kept my hair in place, and my brown-aged work boots tied the whole outfit together. Today, I wasn't an aspiring detective but just a daughter supporting her mother.

As I sat in my room, engrossed in my thoughts, there was a sudden knock at the door that jolted me back to reality. I quickly called out to whoever it was, inviting them in. My brother, Griffin, walked in, looking presentable in his plain black t-shirt, khaki pants, and work boots. He sat at the corner of my bed, and I noticed that he looked deep in thought. "Hey, what's up? I was just about to head downstairs," I said, trying to break the silence. Griffin then began to speak, "I've been thinking about the case and the missing puzzle you were talking about. I was wondering where the kids disappeared and where they could've gone." He paused for a moment before continuing, "Back home, we all would just go to the gas station to hang out after school, so there has to be a place where kids would go to hang out and get away from adults."

I pondered his words, realizing that he was right. "You're right, and we can look it up right now," I said, reaching for my phone. "How can you find that out?" Griffin asked, curious to know. "Even though we can't talk with the cops, there has to be a news article about the kids and where the police might have thought they went or where the trail might have gone cold," I explained.

Finally, after some searching, I found an article from the Pinecrest Press that provided some useful information. It stated that the police were following Carlos' trail to a local teen hangout called Stella Creek, just outside of downtown. It also mentioned that Sheriff Davis believed that this was the spot where the two previous victims met their fate. "This is where a search party is currently canvassing the area and searching for any clues about where the kids have run off to," I concluded.

Griffin stood up, his eyes wide with shock, and said, "So we have a last known location but still nothing much to go off from. I wonder why Leo's Dad would think the kids would run away and go to the creek before disappearing." I gazed out the window, lost in thought, before saying, "The reason they couldn't find anything is that someone led them to that location. It's as if someone was leading the police on the wrong trail, knowing they wouldn't find anything."

Griffin's eyes widened as he stood up, exclaiming, "Do you think Leo's Dad led them there on purpose to cover for the kidnappers? No, you think Leo's Dad is the kidnapper!" I raised my hand, trying to calm him down, and said, "I didn't say that because we can't accuse a police officer, who is probably a hero in this town, of abducting kids. We would put ourselves in hot water if we didn't have hard proof. This is just a theory, but we can't rule it out. We can definitely get more information if we go to the creek and maybe talk with the kids there. But first, we are going to take a trip to this flower farm and help Mom land this vendor." My brother sat back down, nodding in agreement, "Well, at least we got some theories floating around. But yeah, let's go make Mom proud." With that, we both headed out of my room and made our way downstairs, ready to take on the day.

As we descended the stairs, we found our mother in the living room, comfortably seated in an armchair and sipping on her coffee. She looked stunning in a white button-down shirt paired with blue jeans and trendy boots that perfectly complemented her outfit. Our mother greeted us with a warm smile and complimented us on our outfits. "Oh, you both look so nice. Thank you for coming with me today. I really appreciate it. We'll be driving for about 30 minutes, but I've heard that the valley is absolutely beautiful," she said.

We both assured her that we were eagerly looking forward to seeing the farm with the best dahlias in the area. "I've never been on a farm before, so this will be awesome. I was hoping my first farm visit would be to see some cows, but flowers are alright,"

Griffin said. Our mother smiled and replied, "Maybe next time, we'll visit a dairy farm. But today, our goal is to land this vendor and get some dahlias for the shop." It was clear that she was determined to make the most of our trip and ensure that we had a great time.

As my Mom and I were preparing for our road trip to the flower farm, she shared some interesting information about the farm. She had looked it up on Google Maps and discovered that it was quite large, covering an area of about 10 acres. From the satellite view, she also noticed a huge pond off to the side of the farm. In addition, she had read some reviews online, and according to them, Lara Wolfkin, the owner of the farm, was considered the best flower farmer in America.

However, I was a bit surprised that we had never heard of her before. While my brother and I were not particularly familiar with the flower industry, our Mom was, and she had never mentioned Lara Wolfkin. Nevertheless, we needed some specific flowers for a project, and if Lara had them, then she was the lady for the job.

As we hurriedly packed some last-minute items, I grabbed my trusty water bottle and a book I had been reading - Harry Potter and the Deathly Hallows by J.K. Rowling, which I was close to finishing. On the other hand, my Mom picked up her sunglasses, a clipboard with a folder and a notepad attached to it, and some sunscreen for everyone. Meanwhile, my brother was more interested in his snacks and entertainment, so he grabbed a bag of Lay's chips, a bottle of water, and his Nintendo Switch, which he could use to play his favorite Pokemon game. Soon enough, we were all in the car, ready to embark on our adventure. The excitement was palpable as we drove off towards the flower farm, eagerly anticipating what lay ahead.

As we drove along, I couldn't help but notice the beautiful scenery around us. We passed by a variety of farms, each with its own unique charm. There were dairy farms with herds of cows grazing peacefully in the fields, chicken farms with flocks of chickens clucking around, and vegetable farms with rows of fresh produce growing in the soil. The tranquility of the countryside was a stark contrast to the hustle and bustle of the city. I couldn't help but appreciate the wide open spaces and the peace that came with it. It was a refreshing change from the cramped and crowded city life back in New Mexico. As I sat comfortably in the car, I rolled down the windows to take in the awe-inspiring beauty of the lush green fields that stretched out as far as the eye could see. The sweet scent of the surrounding trees filled my nostrils, evoking a sense of peace and tranquility. The vibrant colors of the grass looked so inviting and soft that I couldn't help but imagine how it would feel to run my fingers through it. I longed for the chance to lie back against a nearby tree and bask in the natural beauty surrounding me. In the distance, I gazed with wonder at the breathtaking view of the majestic grey mountains, with peaks that seemed almost surreal, as if they were plucked straight from a Hollywood blockbuster. The sheer size and grandeur of the mountains left me in awe, and I couldn't help but feel humbled by the power of nature.

As our car made its way up the winding road leading to the peak of the ridge, my brother Griffin broke the silence with a question that caught us off guard. "Hey, Mom, is there anything going on between you and That Leo guy?" he asked, his tone curious yet apprehensive. My Mom's face turned beet red, and she replied, "No, why would you say that, Griffin?" But we all knew that there was something more to this question than just simple curiosity.

Griffin looked at me, then turned back to Mom and said, "The other day, when we were about to head to the flower shop, I heard you talking on the phone with someone named Leo. You were talking low, but I could hear you say his name." At this point, my attention turned to my Mom, and I could see that she was clearly embarrassed, with sweat starting to form on her brow.

"He was just calling to see how we all were doing, that's all," my Mom said, trying to diffuse the tension. "Leo and I are just friends, okay? Are you two?" My brother and I nodded, but we both knew that there was something more going on. If my

Mom and Leo were just friends, there wouldn't be any reason to worry. But something about Leo didn't sit right with me. I had a feeling that he was hiding something, and it might be connected to the mysterious disappearance of those kids. I don't have any concrete proof yet, but I'm determined to find out the truth.

As we were descending through the valley after reaching the peak, we were left awestruck by the breathtaking scenery that unfolded before us. The sight of the valley from the top was nothing short of a painter's masterpiece. The high mountainside sloped down to the valley, creating a stunning emerald shape that was simply mesmerizing. The river that meandered through the valley was crystal-clear and shone brighter than anything, reflecting the sunlight that filtered through the clouds. As we made our way down the road, the river flowed alongside us, its serene waters adding to the beauty of the valley. The lush, bright emerald-green grass was a sight to behold, and we could see sheep grazing on it. As we moved further down, the mountains seemed to disappear into the fluffy white clouds that hung over us, leaving only a narrow sliver of sunlight to illuminate the valley.

We spotted a large barn-like house in the distance, with a few small buildings behind it. From afar, we saw colorful flags waving in the wind, which, upon closer inspection, turned out to be flowers of every hue. The sheer number of flowers was overwhelming, and it was hard to comprehend the endless rainbow of colors that stretched before us. Beyond the field of flowers, a dense treeline shielded the area behind it, and the trees looked like guardians of a hidden world. An iron fence ran along the treeline, and it looked indestructible like it would take a bulldozer to break it down. But nothing could hide the massive lake that stretched out behind the property. The lake was much larger than what we had expected, and it took up the entire bottom half of the valley. A river emerged from the lake and snaked its way through the valley, adding to its charm. As we moved further down the valley, it grew narrower, and the mountains seemed to converge, creating a wall from which the clouds could descend. But there was no mistaking that this was the famous Wolfkin Farm that we had been searching for.

As we drove closer to the farm, I couldn't help but notice the various small buildings scattered around the property. They turned out to be carports, providing shelter to several cars parked underneath them. The carports offered protection from the weather in case anything unexpected occurred. To my surprise, the field of flowers we had seen earlier was a vast half-acre field of roses and lilies in different colors. It seemed like a display for visitors to admire as they approached the farm.

As we approached the giant iron gate, we noticed a small metal box with a red button and a speaker attached to it. We realized that we needed to press the button to gain access to the property. My Mom drove the car up to the box, rolled down her window, and pressed the red button. After a few seconds, a lady's voice came through the speaker, asking us what our business at the farm was.

My Mom informed the lady that we were the Torres and that we had an appointment with Ms. Wolfkin. There was a brief pause, and then the lady welcomed us to Wolfkin Farm. We heard a loud horn, and the gate started to swing open. As we drove forward, we had to pass between two massive oak trees that formed a natural archway and obscured the view of the farm from the outside world. We were amazed when the farm came into view, and my jaw dropped.

As our car slowly made its way down the dusty dirt road, we were amazed by the sheer size of Wolfkin

Farm. The fields were so vast that it seemed like the farm must have been bigger than ten acres. On our left, we saw two small buildings with tan siding and red roofs. Above them, there were signs that read 'Farm Stands.' A small parking lot was situated beside both the buildings. As we approached, we noticed people walking back to their cars carrying bouquets of cut flowers and fruit baskets. It was evident that the farm was a popular destination for the locals to pick up fresh produce and beautiful flowers.

Beyond the buildings, to our left, there were ten fields, each the size of a football field. Each field had a different color of flowers waving in the wind, making it clear that each field was dedicated to a specific type of flower. The closest field to us was a field of roses, and they were the most beautiful roses we had ever seen. The petals shone brightly in the sun, displaying colors that we had only seen in magazines. The colors ranged from red, yellow, orange, white, pink, and coral, which we had never seen in roses before. The other fields were too far for us to see, but we could only imagine how beautiful they must have looked.

To our right, a group of different barns was clustered together, with people moving in and out of them. They were all Latinos who were dressed to work, a familiar sight for us coming from New Mexico. The men wore straw hats with dark sunglasses, long-sleeved shirts, work jeans, and heavy-duty rain boots. The women either wore straw hats or bandanas and were dressed in either normal long sleeves or button-down long sleeves, some in dresses, some in jeans, but all wore rain boots.

As we drove further, my Mom saw a sign that read 'Visitor Parking.' She pulled our car into the gravel-filled parking lot, which was in front of a large barn that was shaped like a "U." The other barns were situated beside this building, and there was a pond next to them that wrapped around the back of the buildings. As we got out of the car and looked around, we were left in awe of everything around us. We had never seen anything like Wolfkin Farm before; it was like a world of its own, and we had only seen a fraction of the place.

We found ourselves standing together by the car, uncertain of what to do next. In the midst of our confusion, a lady dressed in a stunning purple sundress and a stylish straw hat caught our attention. She was taller than both my mother and me, with striking features that matched her height. I could sense that she was in her late forties or early fifties. Her long hair was a blend of salt and pepper, and her skin was a beautiful cream color that exuded elegance. Her arms looked firm and sturdy as if she had been working in the fields for a while. I also noticed an assortment of flower tattoos on her shoulder, which looked lovely. As she approached us, her warm smile extended from ear to ear. She introduced herself as Lara Wolfkin, the owner of Wolfkin Farm.

"Hello, Ms. Wolfkin. My name is Olivia Torres, and these are my children, Hazel and Griffin Torres. It's lovely to meet you," my Mom greeted. Lara shook my Mom's hand and replied, "Oh, just call me Lara. It's nice to meet you all too. I remember we talked on the phone, and you were in the market for some flowers, correct?"

"Yes, I heard you're the only place to get dahlias around here," my Mom said. Lara chuckled and said, "Oh right, I forgot that the other farmers around here won't grow dahlias. I don't know why, but I guess I cornered the market on those." As we continued walking, Lara inquired about our purpose and why we moved here. "So, you're opening a flower shop in Pinecrest? I think that's wonderful, but I've never heard of you guys before. Are you new to town?" she asked.

"Yes, we are new to town. We just moved here the other day from New Mexico," my Mom said. Lara expressed her excitement and then asked about the reason behind the move. "Well, my husband passed away, and I thought it would be good for us to have a fresh start. Also, I've been wanting to open a flower shop forever, and I read that Washington is where the best flowers are grown," my Mom explained.

She then empathized with my Mom's loss and shared her own experience. "Oh, I'm so sorry to hear about your loss. I lost my husband, too; trust me, dear; it gets easier. I hope you'll find success in this new chapter of your life. But I guess you would like to talk more business now, I suppose. Yes, indeed, Washington State is the home of the best flowers in the United States. Let me give you all a tour so you can see more of our operation. Should we start with the educational garden or the flower fields? I'll let you all decide," Lara said. We all agreed that we wanted to see the flower fields first. I know my Mom wanted to see the flowers for the business, but I just wanted to see how the rest of the flowers looked after seeing those stunning roses.

As we walked from the car to the flower fields, Lara gave us a detailed history of the farm. She explained that Wolfkin Farm had been around for 30 years and that she had started it when she was about 23 years old. Lara and her husband had purchased the land from an old sheep farmer who was retiring. They put all of their life savings into buying the place and, after taking out a few loans, were able to build the farm that we see today. It was impressive to learn how she turned a sheep farm into a high-end flower farm.

Lara then shared that the sheep still hung around the farm, grazing on the grass in the valley. She thought that the sheep would all disappear, but they still stuck around, adding a rustic charm to the place. We finally made it to the huge acreage of flower fields, where Lara explained that there were ten different fields, each housing one type of flower. The fields were boxed in like rectangles with dirt roads separating them.

Before we continued walking, Lara told us that Wolfkin Farm only grew ten types of flowers: Dahlias, Roses, Peonies, Lilies, Sunflowers, Gladiolus, Zinnias, Cosmos, Snapdragons, and Sweet Peas. She explained that she would grow more, but she wants to keep the number small so they can grow the best quality flowers. Even though she only grew ten different flowers, I still think that having one football-sized area dedicated to one flower is still a lot.

We reached the base of the fields, where we saw the rose field to the right and the Lilies to the left. Lara then surprised us by saying she had already contacted one of her workers, Jorge, to give us a tour of the golf cart. As she said that, a lanky man wearing a straw hat, blue long-sleeve button-down, work jeans, and leather cowboy boots pulled up in a golf cart. Lara introduced him as Jorge, the head maintenance man of the whole farm. He smiled at us and waved. It was hard to see his smile because of his huge salt-and-pepper-colored mustache. I assumed he had to be in his 50s, but he looked strong, and confidence radiated off of him. Jorge then motioned us to join him in the six-person golf cart. Lara and my Mom sat behind him, while Griffin and I sat in the last row of seats behind them. Once we were all seated and strapped in, the tour began.

When we entered the farm, our attention was immediately drawn to the roses. However, we were eager to explore the rest of the property, so Jorge kindly offered to take us around each plot. Our first stop was the peony field, and it was a sight to behold! As far as the eye could see, rows upon rows of peonies filled the entire space. Each peony sat atop a long, dark green stem that seemed to stretch towards the sky, showcasing its beauty at the top. Some peony bulbs were closed and shaped like small baseballs, while others that we saw the worker harvesting were fully bloomed, spreading their petals out like confetti. The vast array of different colors took our breath away as we gazed at the white, pink, yellow, black, red, purple, and blue peonies. The petals were so soft and delicate, yet so vivid and vibrant. Jorge kept the golf cart at a slow speed, knowing that we were all lost in the beauty of the peonies.

Eventually, Jorge drove on, and we made a left to reach the edge of the lily fields. The lilies were a showstopper. My brother Griffin and I looked at each other, saying how the field of lilies looked like colorful starfish floating in the air. Each lily was more magnificent than the rest. The bloom spread in a full star, displaying an array of colors that were highlighted by the sun. No single lily was a solid color; some were pink with white edges, blood red with pink edges, or even a fully white lily with a yellow hue in the center. We could see each worker handling the blooms with such care as if they were carrying a star.

As Jorge turned around the corner, we spotted a vast field of towering sunflowers. The sunflowers looked like an ordinary variety, with their large black center filled with sunflower seeds and yellow petals resembling the sun. However, there was something different about these sunflowers - they were enormous, standing tall at ten to fifteen feet and boasting stems as wide as my arm. It was as though a giant had planted these flowers for decoration on his coffee table. We saw a worker carrying a large backpack that looked like a sack. They held a pair of shears in their hand, and every time they cut a sunflower down, they would place the stem-first into their sack. One of the workers had already collected enough sunflowers in his bag that it created an overlooking shadow, keeping him cool in the shade. Lara explained that they had used a special fertilizer that worked too well, making these sunflowers gigantic.

Lara then directed Jorge to drive us to the gladiolus field. As we arrived, it felt like we had stepped into a cartoon world. The gladiolus flowers had a single stem, with multiple flowers descending down the stem, almost resembling little stars stacked on top of each other. The colors were overwhelming, with shades of red, blue, yellow, white, purple, orange, and every other color on the rainbow. It was like a sea of colors, with no two colors staying next to each other. The entire field looked like a burst of colors, as though it had exploded everywhere. I asked Lara about the colors, and she said that they could be overwhelming, but eventually, one would get used to them. She then guided Jorge towards the zinnias.

Zinnias were my brother Griffin's favorite, as he loved how simple they looked and how the petals made the flower appear like a colorful planet. As Jorge pulled to a slow stop overlooking the zinnia fields, my brother nearly jumped out of his seat. A rainbow sea of different colored planets greeted him, and I had to hold him back down. He said he had never imagined seeing so many different colored zinnias in a single place. I had to admit that even though the flower looked simple, it had its charm, making me want to get closer to it. Lara mentioned that zinnias paired well with peonies when making bouquets, as they helped fill each other out.

As Lara explained more about the benefits of having zinnias in bouquets, she instructed Jorge to drive over to the cosmos to see another flower she used to fill bouquets. The cosmos were similar to regular flowers, but Lara said that they were great additions to other flowers. She explained that the cosmos don't work well by themselves. Lara then pointed to a field next to the cosmos, where we saw Snapdragon flowers. They looked like gladiolus, but the blooms did not descend. Instead, they bunched together and spread in a bulging mass around the stem of the plant. Each Snapdragon flower had a different color combination, just like the lilies. Some blooms had white petals with a bright red center, while others had a light purple bloom with a darker shade of purple in the middle. Lara explained that some customers prefer gladiolus while others prefer snapdragons. Therefore, she grows both.

Lastly, Jorge drove us to a field that had 30 different log rows with a fence running down each one. The fence was covered in vines that climbed all over it, with little pods that looked like sweet peas. My brother asked if he could eat one, and Lara suggested he could, but it wouldn't taste good. He tried one anyway and spat it out just as fast as he ate it. We all laughed. Lara explained that these were sweet pea flowers, and she doesn't eat the pods but instead uses the vines with the flowers to make wreaths and other side projects. As we looked up, we saw shattered blooms all over the fence in red, pink, white, and blue colors. It is a solid plant for spring

wreath making and maybe something to eat if you are hungry enough.

Lara said, "We have more than just
flowers on this farm. Let me show you
our orchard. Our fruit trees do very
well this time of year." Jorge drove the
golf cart to the back of the farm, and
we approached a wall of trees with a
sweet smell of fruit in the air. As we
got closer, I could see the bright red
apples hanging from the trees, shining brightly in the sun. The bright
red was a perfect complement to the
bright, lush green leaves of the tree.
Jorge stopped the golf cart in front
of the apple tree so we could all get
out and stretch our legs a bit. "These
are our apple trees, and if you look

further back, you'll see some cherry, pear, peaches, plum, and apricot trees," Lara said. "Why do you have so many trees if this is a flower farm?" my brother asked. "Well, flowers don't grow year-round, and it's nice to have another income source to help make up for the slow times. Also, these trees provide great protection from the wind for our flowers," Lara explained. "I have a question, too. When we drove down into the valley, we saw the massive lake behind the property, but this whole time, we hadn't seen it once. Where did it go?" I asked.

Lara turned to Jorge and asked if he could do us a favor by picking some ripe apples from the tree. Without hesitation, Jorge fetched a ladder from the nearby shed and carefully positioned it against the tree. With expert precision, he ascended the ladder and reached for the nearest branch. After picking a handful of apples, he descended and distributed them to each of us. As I held the apple in my hand, its vibrant color and smooth texture captivated me. Upon taking a bite, an explosion of sweetness enveloped my senses, surpassing even the delectable cookies baked by Evelyn. Lara, taking a bite of her own apple, remarked, "The lake serves as our primary water source. If you look beyond the trees, you can catch a glimpse of it." Peering through the foliage, I spotted the glistening surface of the blue lake in the distance. "Next time, with more time on our hands, I'll take you all to the lake. For now, let's return to the main house and continue our discussion in the educational garden," Lara suggested.

We all hopped back into the golf cart, and Jorge skillfully drove us back toward the area where we had parked our cars. After a short ride, we found ourselves near the imposing U-shaped building. Jorge guided us behind the building to an open space filled with various project areas. As we explored, we encountered a sign that indicated an event space, marking an open field encircled by trees. Nearby, another sign pointed to a compost area, where workers were busy depositing dead flowers and weeds into open stalls for decomposition.

Our final stop was the education garden, located in the farthest area. Jorge expertly maneuvered the golf cart to the entrance, which was marked by two rose bushes serving as a charming walkway. The garden itself spanned about a quarter of an acre and was bursting with a diverse array of flowers. Scattered throughout the garden were stone tables and benches, providing tranquil spots for

visitors to sit and admire the surroundings.

"This is the education garden where we conduct classes about the flowers we grow, and we hope to teach others how to care for their own flowers," Lara explained. After bidding Jorge farewell as he went off to attend to his other duties, my Mom expressed her admiration for the garden and mentioned her interest in attending Lara's next class.

Lara, however, regretfully shared that she was pressed for time and redirected our attention to the matter at hand. As we settled at one of the stone tables, I couldn't help but marvel at Lara's accomplishments.

It made me hopeful that my Mom would achieve similar success in the future. Throughout the tour, something nagged at me. Despite their smiles, none of the workers we encountered seemed genuinely happy. Even though Jorge had appeared cheerful, I sensed an underlying discontent. I couldn't shake off the feeling and began to wonder about the reasons behind their apparent lack of happiness.

Sitting in the educational garden was very relaxing, especially being surrounded by fragrant peonies. I felt a sense of calm as my Mom and Lara delved into their business discussion.

My younger brother Griffin, restless as always, decided to explore the lush garden instead of staying in place. I couldn't blame him; the intricate details of flower farming weren't exactly riveting for a young boy.

Lara, taking the lead, initiated the conversation by asking, "Now that you've had a chance to see everything my farm has to offer, which flowers are you interested in?" My Mom replied, "Everything looks amazing, but we're specifically looking for dahlias at the moment." Lara explained, "I have a wide variety of dahlias grown in a separate section of the farm due to their unique requirements. I'm sorry we didn't have time to show you those. What type of dahlias are you looking for?"

Impressed by Lara's offerings, my Mom responded, "After seeing your farm, I'm sure your dahlias are exceptional. We're particularly interested in Ball Dahlias. Will you have any available for next week?" Lara replied, "Ah, I see you're preparing for the shop opening. I certainly have Ball Dahlias ready for you." With that, Lara pulled out her phone and began listing the various types of dahlias she had available.

Lara provided a detailed list of the various flowers available, including Peaches n Cream, Cornel Red, Cornel Bronzer, Jowie Winnie, Sweet Natalie, Jomamda, Bloomquist, Cozytown, and several others. After reviewing the options, my Mom expressed interest in Cozytown, Jowie Winnie, Sweet Natalie, Peaches n Cream, and Cornel Red. She inquired if it would be possible to have these flowers prepared by the following week. Lara confirmed that it would not be a problem and quoted a price of $50 per bundle, with each bundle containing approximately 15 to 20 flowers. However, she mentioned that they only accept checks and cash, and orders would need to be picked up from the headhouse, as they do not offer delivery services. Upon finalizing the order for two bundles of each variety, Lara assured my Mom that she would receive an email notification once the flowers were ready for pickup. The exchange concluded with mutual anticipation for their future collaboration as my Mom extended her hand across the table to shake Lara's hand.

As we all rose from the stone table, I couldn't help but notice a massive stone chimney extending from the back of the house, seemingly leading down to a basement. Adjacent to the chimney were grand wooden double doors also leading to the basement. "Hey Lara, what's the purpose of that enormous chimney?" I inquired. Lara turned to me with intense eyes, almost as if she didn't want me to bring it up. "Oh, that's where I produce my homemade fertilizer. I like to combine Osmocote with a few other ingredients to create my own special blend," she replied. Her words didn't quite match her reaction; it was evident that she didn't want to elaborate, but I managed to get her talking, so I decided to press further. "Wow, you make your own fertilizer? That's fascinating. What other ingredients do you mix with Osmocote, as you mentioned?" I probed. Lara seemed even more hesitant to entertain my follow-up question. "Now, dear, that's a secret I can't divulge. Olivia, it was lovely meeting all of you. I hope you have a safe journey, and we'll be in touch."

Lara ended the conversation and walked away before I could ask more questions. Maybe it's the detective inside of me, but something wasn't right about that exchange. How did a question about a chimney get someone so upset? Well, maybe it's her secret blend, and she doesn't want people to know. Maybe it's something she holds dear, so she's overprotective about it. Either way, mission accomplished. We got the dahlias, and now my Mom will have the flowers she needs for the shop's grand opening. My Mom told Griffin we were leaving, and he ran over from some lilies he was face-deep in. "You really liked those lilies?" I asked Griffin. "I've never smelled anything like that before. Mom, did you make the deal?" Griffin asked our Mom. "Yep, we got what we came for and can head home now," my Mom said.

As we strolled back around the U-shaped building to return to our car, my Mom informed me and Griffin that, for the time being, we would need to drive here to pick up the flowers until she could hire employees. I reassured her that it was fine by me, and my brother also agreed. After we all loaded up in the car, as my Mom started to back up and pull forward towards the gates, I noticed some of the workers giving us the saddest looks. It made me wonder if they even wanted to be there or if this was their only option for employment. Something didn't sit right with me. Maybe it was just my imagination, but Wolfkin Farm might be too good to be true.

Chapter Six
Stella Creek

As we drove home from the farm, I found myself lost in thought. The passing trees outside the window seemed to have a calming effect, allowing me to clear my mind. There was already so much on my plate - adjusting to the move from New Mexico, finding my place in the new town, helping my Mom with her flower shop, and being there for my brother as he struggled to adapt. I could sense that leaving his old life behind had been tough on him, even though he tried to hide it. But working on this case seemed to bring out something new in him.

The case of the missing children weighed heavily on my mind. Despite my Mom's warnings, I couldn't shake the feeling that I needed to get involved. Maybe part of it was a selfish desire to prove myself beyond the small-town success of solving the missing cat case. But there was more to it than that. The faces of those kids haunted me, and I couldn't bear the thought of their lives being forgotten just because they were orphans.

And then there was Leo. Something about him didn't sit right with me. It wasn't just the fact that he seemed to have a thing going on with my Mom. It was the realization that he and his father had been involved in covering up a case that had remained unsolved for over 25 years. There was definitely more to this than met the eye. The spun narrative is that the kids disappeared because they ran away and got lost in the woods. Any normal person could see that the kids were being kidnapped, but I guess when you're the police of a small town, people will just follow whatever story you give them.

After a peaceful moment, my Mom broke the silence and inquired, "How did you guys like the farm?" I snapped back to reality and replied, "The place was absolutely stunning, but there was something about that Lara lady that didn't sit right with me." Griffin, engrossed in his game in the backseat, not paying attention, intermittently muttered phrases like "got him" or "one more attack," indicating that he was doing just fine.

"Lara seemed lovely to me. Why do you feel something was off about her?" my Mom asked. "Well, everything was fine until I brought up the topic of the chimney," I explained. "I think she was just protective of her special fertilizer. But that's not enough to form a negative opinion about someone," my Mom reasoned.

"I understand that, but I also couldn't shake the feeling when I saw how unhappy her workers looked as we were leaving," I added. "I noticed that too. They put on a brave face during the tour, but once we were out of sight, I could see the sadness in their eyes. Our people work tirelessly and barely receive the appreciation they deserve. I remember your father working as hard as four men, only for someone else to take credit. It's a harsh reality, but that's the world we live in. I hate to say it, but we have to look out for ourselves. I know it's difficult to witness, but we need Lara's flowers for the shop to thrive," my Mom explained.

Understanding my Mom's perspective, I reflected on how hard my dad used to work, and I found myself relating more to Lara Wolfkin's workers. However, I knew I had to separate my personal feelings and focus on my family. "I understand, Mom, and I believe the shop will be a great success," I assured her. "I have the same feeling, but I also feel my stomach growling," Griffin chimed in from the backseat. My Mom and I exchanged amused glances and burst into laughter. "Alright, Griffin, I'll prepare a hearty meal for us when we get home," my Mom promised.

After returning home and having a hearty dinner, Griffin and I headed back up to the attic to delve deeper into the case. Griffin sat at the table, meticulously jotting down notes based on the news article we had read earlier that day. We knew that the police were focusing their search on Stella Creek as the suspected location where the missing kids might have gone. It was a small piece of the puzzle, but it was better than nothing. As I stared at the board, I couldn't help but wonder if there were any specific physical features or traits shared by the missing kids that might have made them targets for the kidnappers. However, none of them seemed to have anything in common. I also delved into each of their backgrounds, scouring public records online, and discovered that none of the kids came from the same place or had similar backgrounds. It felt like another dead end in our search.

"Griffin, could you do me a favor and grab my phone? I need to find out more about Stella Creek. It's our only lead at the moment," I requested. Griffin picked up my phone and performed a Google search on Stella Creek. "It looks like it's just a local hangout spot for teenagers. But it's strange that the kid would disappear so close to downtown without anyone noticing. There's one more lead we can follow - we could check out the orphanage," Griffin suggested. "I understand, but I think we should start with the last known location. It might provide us with more information so we can ask better questions later. Besides, we might encounter fewer obstacles there. We can figure out a way to approach the orphanage later, but for now, let's head to the creek," I responded.

I will admit that my little brother is impressing me with his skills. He's only 12 years old, but he already knows exactly what questions to ask and what to look for when researching. It's really impressive. I wish Dad could see him now; he would be so proud. "What do you think we should look for when we go by the creek?" I asked. "Well, I've been reading a lot of Sherlock Holmes books, and if I were in his shoes, I would check for clues to see if there are places where the kids could have gotten lost, like a secret trail or something. Then, I hope there are some other kids around so we can ask them more about the creek, and maybe they might know more about the kids that went missing. You know, If Sherlock was on this case, he would probably ask why a place where five kids disappeared would still be open to the public. I would think it would be closed off," Griffin said.

Now I know where Dad's Sherlock Holmes collection went. I was looking all over for it, but I guess Griffin had it this whole time. No wonder he's been improving so well. "I think those are excellent clues to look for. If it is a popular hangout spot, there are going to be other kids there. They might give us more insight than what the adults will tell us. But it's getting late, and we've got to help Mom tomorrow at the flower shop, so we should go get some sleep. We'll pick this back up tomorrow when we have time."

As I said this, Griffin let out a big yawn and agreed it was time for bed. He stood up and headed down the attic stairs. I packed up some of the notes and put them in a binder so we knew where they were. I walked over to the door and looked back at the board with the missing kids' posters. This was starting to become a habit, and before I left the room, I always looked at the posters. Maybe it was something in me that reminded me I was doing this for them. I turned off the light and headed downstairs for bed.

As we woke up the next morning, we prepared to head to the flower shop. I assumed we might be help-ing out with some cleaning while my Mom was occupied on the phone, but I wasn't entirely certain. The drive into town was always a pleasant experience. Since it was early, each coffee shop we passed had a long line of eager customers in need of their morning fix. Upon arriving at the flower shop, my Mom parked the car by the curb, and we all stepped out. Just as I was about to head towards the entrance, my Mom surprised me and Griffin by saying that she didn't really need our help that day and encouraged us to explore the town instead. She explained that she would be tied up on the phone all day and told us to give her a call if we needed anything.

I told my Mom that Griffin and I would be safe and that I would have my phone with me in case of any emergency. As she walked into the flower shop, I turned to Griffin and asked if he was thinking what I was thinking. He suggested heading to the creek while we had the chance. I agreed but suggested that we first look up the directions so we wouldn't waste time wandering around. I took out my phone and searched for directions to Stella Creek. After a quick search, I found that if we walked down to Jubilee Avenue and kept straight, there would be a sign at the end of the road leading to a trail that would take us to the creek. I asked Griffin if he was ready to go, and with a big grin on his face, he nodded eagerly. We set off on our adventure.

As we leisurely walked down the bustling sidewalk toward Jubilee Avenue, we passed by a variety of shops and apartments. One particular place that caught our eye was Tommy's Tools, a well-stocked hardware store showcasing an impressive array of screwdrivers, wrenches, saws, and hammers in its window display. Continuing our stroll, we reached Pinecrest Ice Cream Wonders, where a delightful presentation of faux ice cream cones filled with a colorful assortment of flavors greeted us. Behind the counter, we observed the diligent staff diligently preparing for the day, carefully filling buckets with generous scoops of creamy ice cream. Despite Griffin's longing for a sweet treat, I gently explained that it was too early in the morning and reassured him that we could indulge later. Secretly, I also grappled with the reality that I didn't have any money to spare for ice cream right now.

We had finally reached Jubilee Avenue, and as we turned down the road, we couldn't help but notice that it led straight into the woods. At the end of the road, a sign with a strikingly bright red arrow caught our attention, pointing and declaring, "This way to Stella Creek." Sensing the potential adventure ahead, I turned to

Griffin and emphasized the need to stay alert for any clues that might come our way. Just as we were about to set off, a familiar voice called out to us from behind. I turned around to find Miles waving enthusiastically at us. His siblings, Lucas and Ava, were standing beside him. Miles was lugging a cooler in each hand, while Lucas had an umbrella and some blankets. Meanwhile, Ava was clutching a vibrant beach ball. Dressed as if they were headed for a beach day, in swim trunks and tank tops, it was evident that they were well-prepared for the outdoors, complete with visible sunscreen to shield themselves from the sun's rays.

"Hey, Miles, long time no see. How have you been?" I greeted him as they crossed the street. "Hey, it has been a couple of days, hasn't it? We've been busy helping our Mom get the flower shop ready," I explained. Griffin and Lucas exchanged a competitive glance, clearly eager to resume their interrupted basketball game. "I think we still have a basketball game to finish," Lucas declared. Griffin teased, "I hope your jumper has gotten better since the last time we played." Lucas retorted, "My jump shot was enough for you last time." Griffin chuckled, "It was enough to make you fall behind if I remembered correctly." The tension diffused as they laughed and exchanged a high-five. "Boys are stupid," Ava remarked while standing next to me. I complimented her beach ball, and she flashed a smile in return.

"Are you guys heading to the creek?" Miles asked. I didn't want to let them know what we were really up to, so I said, "Yeah, we didn't have to help our Mom today, so we wanted to check out the creek we've been hearing about. I read somewhere that this was the local hangout spot," I said. Miles and his sibling looked at each other with confused looks. "Who told you that? Barely anyone ever comes to the creek," Lucas said. Griffin and I looked at each other. "But we heard that this is where all the kids go to hang out. I read in the newspaper that it was a popular spot in town," Griffin said. "The newspaper? Why are you reading the newspaper? Are you an old man now, Griffin? I guess that's why you don't want to play me in basketball because you might break a hip," Lucas said while laughing. "I'll take you on anytime, Lucas!" Griffin shouted. "Enough, Lucas, leave him alone. But just so you guys know, the local newspaper never tells the complete truth about what goes on in town. They just repeat what people tell them. The creek is a fun spot for us because we like to have a picnic and play in the water. We're from California, so we miss the beaches, and the creek is the closest thing we have to that. But as long as we've been here, hardly anyone comes to the creek," Miles said. "Is it because of the kids disappearing?" I asked. "No, it's not because of that. As far as I can tell, most of the people that live here are just a bunch of hipsters who like to hang out at the coffee shop," Miles said. I looked down, thinking that everything we had read could have possibly been a lie this whole time. So that might explain how the police were able to spin the narrative because all they had to do was tell the newspaper what they wanted and they just ran with it.

Miles asked, "Do you two want to join us? We've got plenty of sodas and sandwiches." I said we would love to join them but asked for a minute to let our Mom know where we were going. Miles said they would meet us down there, and he and his sibling made their way toward Stella Creek. "Well, that was a big surprise. Should we stick to the game plan and look for clues?" Griffin asked. "No, change of plans. We are going to ask our new friends what else they might know. See what you can get out of Lucas, and I'll work on Miles. Ava might know something, too," I said. We both agreed to the new plan and made our way towards Stella Creek.

Walking down the narrow trail was pleasant. The wind whistling through the trees was a nice sound that made me feel relaxed, even though we were walking to a place where kids had supposedly gone missing. Just up ahead was the clearing leading out to the creek. Griffin and Lucas were talking about Pokémon cards and what they had to trade. Ava was holding my hand and telling me more about California and how they would always go to the beach on the weekends. Miles was leading the way and would occasionally look back and smile. It was a nice feeling just walking and hanging out with other people. It almost made me feel normal, but in the back of my mind, I kept thinking about the case and that we still had a job to do.

As we leisurely walked through the open space, the soft, golden rays of the sun enveloped the stunning panorama of the stream in a welcoming warmth. The earthy trail led us from the protection of the trees to a rugged shoreline embellished with a striking assortment of gray and white stones. Across the stream, a rocky bank was flanked by towering trees that provided ample shade. The shallow, translucent waters unveiled polished gray rocks beneath the surface. The creek's length seemed immeasurable as it wound out of sight in both directions, concealed by the dense, verdant foliage. Coming from a more city-like environment, this encounter with natural beauty was profoundly enlightening for me.

As I stood by the clear water, I couldn't help but marvel at the stunning scenery. "Wow, this place is amazing. The water is so clear, I can actually see the rocks," I exclaimed. Miles, who had been here before, nodded in agreement. "Yeah, when we first came here, it was breathtaking for me too. I've been hiking with my Dad, and we've seen plenty of creeks, but this one takes the cake," he said. After setting up our picnic spot, Miles and I settled down on the blankets while Griffin, Lucas, and Ava headed toward the water to play. Griffin shot me a knowing look, silently communicating that we should keep an eye out for clues as we played. Miles handed me a bottle of root beer as he set up the umbrella for shade. Although I suggested sitting closer to the trees, he insisted on being close to Ava in case she needed help. It was clear that he deeply cared for his siblings. As we sipped our drinks, the tranquil sound of the flowing water mixed with the laughter of the kids, creating a perfect afternoon.

I put down my soda and pondered silently, "How can I encourage Miles to share more about what he knows without coming across as intrusive?" I certainly didn't want to give the impression that I wasn't interested in getting to know him. Throughout our interaction, he had been consistently kind and respectful to me. Even as he sat beside me, he maintained a respectful distance, never encroaching on my personal space but still close enough for us to engage in conversation. His attention was divided as he periodically glanced at the water to ensure the safety of his siblings. It was endearing in its own way. I would like to learn more about Miles at a later time, as opportunities like this might not present themselves again anytime soon.

As Miles and I sat by the creek, I asked him, "Apart from the creek, what do you enjoy about this town?" Setting down his soda, Miles replied, "The creek is definitely my favorite thing here, but I also appreciate how friendly everyone is. When I first arrived, I was struck by the number of local shops. It felt like stepping into a time machine, especially coming from areas filled with big retail chains like Walmart and Target." Taking another sip of my soda, I chimed in, "I had the same feeling when we moved into our new house." Miles reached into the cooler and grabbed a turkey sandwich, asking about life in New Mexico. "We didn't live in a fancy neighborhood, but it was a tight-knit community. We all looked out for each other. When my Dad passed away, I remember the out-pouring of support from our neigh-bors. They lined up outside our door, bringing food and offering their con-dolences," I recounted. "I'm truly sor-ry to hear about your dad. I can't imagine how difficult that must have been," Miles expressed. "We're cop-ing as best as we can, which is why we decided to start fresh here. I miss him a lot; we used to watch a ton of detec-tive movies together. He had a knack for solving mysteries and would often figure out the culprit before the movie ended. If he had his way, I think he would have pursued a career as a detective."

"Your dad sounds really cool. Did the detective bug bite you, too?" Miles asked. I laughed, thinking about what he said. "Haha, I guess you could say that. I hope to be a detective one day, but I still have a long way to go. My brother got bitten too recently; he's been reading my dad's Sherlock Holmes books and really getting into the mystery-solving business." Miles smiled and took another sip from his root beer. Maybe this would be the best time to ask now that we've let our guard down. "Hey, speaking of mystery, Griffin and I have been looking into what happened to those missing kids. Do you know anything about what really happened? I know the police think the kids ran away, but there's no way that really happened," I said. Miles put his soda back down on the ground and looked off into the distance. "I'm glad we're not the only ones who don't trust the police," Miles said.

"What do you mean by that?" I asked Miles. He looked upset, but he said, "Five years ago, I lost a really good friend. Her name was Linh. She was an orphan, but she was my best friend. We met by accident at the library when she got lost from her reading group, going to the boys' bathroom by mistake. It was a shock seeing her walk in, but we had a good laugh about it. Once a week, a group of kids from the orphanage would visit the library, and that's when we would meet up. She was great, and I think she would have gotten adopted soon. A lot of families would come and visit her. I think she would have made it. But then, the day that her group was supposed to come to the library, she wasn't with them. I asked the counselor where she was, and they told me she had gone missing. A week later, the newspaper reported that she went missing, and the police lost her trail here at the creek. When I said she must have been kidnapped, everyone told me the police said she ran away. I argued that it didn't make sense because she would have been adopted soon, but I got shut down and was told that I had to trust the police and what they said. But I didn't believe that nonsense. They told the same story with the last four kids, and I couldn't believe that people would still just listen to the same old story all over again. But I guess because they were orphans, it wasn't a big deal. That's what messed up about people. They only care about their own problems. I miss Linh, and I wish I could have done more, but I'm not the detective type like you and your family. Are you really looking into it?" Miles said.

"I'm sorry to hear that, Miles. But we are looking into it. When I was at the police station and saw the posters, something came over me like I had to solve this case. I pieced together that the police had to be spinning the narrative, but I couldn't prove it. I also believe that they were kidnapped. It didn't make sense to me that they would just run away. But now, after what you just told me, I truly believe that Detective Leo is definitely hiding something," I said. I looked over at Miles, and he was red with anger. I asked if he was okay. He took a deep breath and said, "Don't say that guy's name around me. I might not be a detective, but he was the one that took Linh. I know it." I was stunned. Did he really just say that? "Do you have proof?" I asked. "No, I don't, but Linh would talk about how creepy he was and how he would always take her to places and tell her not to tell anyone because it was their special place," Miles said. I began to feel disturbed by what he said. "What was he doing with her?" I asked. "I don't know, but she would always try to get out of going with him, but the orphanage thought that she was just being difficult. I was too young to know better, but I should have told my parents. Maybe they could have done something," Miles said. "Wait, why was he picking her up and taking her places? Wouldn't the orphanage stop a grown man from taking a little girl on day trips?" I asked. "Normally, yes, but every kid at the orphanage was in a mentor program run by the police. Leo was her mentor, and another reason why I believe he took her was because this creek was one of their special places."

Griffin, Lucas, and Ava emerged from the water and joined Miles on the blanket while I sat with an umbrella to provide some shade. Lucas and Ava were completely soaked, but Griffin managed to stay relatively dry. As they settled in, I offered them root beer from the cooler. In a hushed tone, Griffin asked if I had discovered anything, to which I replied that I would brief him later. "Miles, is the orphanage called Hope's Refuge?" I inquired. He said yes and mentioned that it was on the other side of Downtown, about a twenty-minute walk from our here. He told us to head straight down Main Street and make a right at the "Welcome to Downtown" sign. Expressing gratitude, I shared that we needed to leave. Although Lucas and Ava seemed puzzled, Miles wore a warm smile and wished us luck.

Me and Griffin slowly made our way back to the trail that wound through the dense forest, leading us back to downtown. I filled him in on every detail of my conversation with Miles, watching as a troubled expression settled on his young face. Despite being only twelve, he managed to collect himself after hearing the unsettling news. "We need to head to the Orphanage and ask more questions," I suggested. Griffin fell silent for a few moments, and I thought he had regained his composure. However, it was clear that the weight of the situation was still bearing down on him.

I asked him if he was okay, and his response only heightened my concern. "That Leo guy is really bad news, and I'm afraid he's going to do something to Mom," Griffin confessed. We halted our walk, and I knelt down to his eye level, trying to provide reassurance. "We are going to do everything in our power to ensure he will never hurt anyone ever again, especially Mom," I promised. Wiping his eyes, he managed a small smile. Standing up, I took his hand, and we resumed our journey with a renewed sense of determination.

The situation has escalated more than I expected. What initially seemed like a simple case has become increasingly complex with each new discovery. Normally, I would suggest involving the police, but the issue lies with the local law enforcement. The small-town environment seems to have allowed the police department to lie without being held accountable. Perhaps seeking help from the neighboring town's police could be an option, but their jurisdiction might limit their ability to intervene. Contacting the FBI is another consideration, but their lack of action so far is concerning. It looks like it's up to us to uncover evidence that Detective Leo and his father have been dishonest about the children's situation. However, I must also ensure Griffin's safety, as he remains a prime target for our suspect.

Chapter Seven
Hope's Refuge

As we walked through down-town, my surroundings seemed like a blur. The shops and buildings passed by, but I couldn't focus on any of them. I was lost in my thoughts, consumed by the fear of Leo's po-tential danger. My mind raced with worries about the threat he posed to my brother and mother. When we reached the end of Main Street and turned the corner, Hope's Refuge, the Orphanage where the missing kids lived, came into view. I stopped in my tracks, overwhelmed by the realization that we had no one to turn to for help. What if I was in over my head? What if I couldn't uncover the truth or expose Leo for his actions? I hadn't proven that Leo took the kids; it was all speculation. Yet, deep down, I felt certain that he was responsible. The questions swirled in my mind - why did he take the kids? Where could he have taken them? What did he want from them, or worse, what did he do to them? The weight of these unanswered questions pressed down on me, and the thought of leading my little brother, Griffin, into danger was unbearable. The suffocating pressure of solving this case made it hard to breathe as the weight of everything began to burden my shoulders.

As my mind was consumed with thoughts, Griffin's tug on my arm brought me back to the present. He looked at me with concern and asked, "Hey Hazel, are you okay? The Orphanage is right there. What's the game plan?" I met his determined gaze and realized I couldn't afford to let doubt take over. We were a team, and my brother's unwavering resolve despite understanding the danger gave me the courage I needed. "We need a cover story," I replied, taking out my phone and opening the notes app to make it look like I was doing some research.

"Why do we need a cover story? We're just going to ask some questions," Griffin inquired, puzzled by my actions. I continued typing on my phone, trying to make it look convincing. "What are you doing on your phone, Hazel? This is serious. Are you texting Miles?" Griffin's suspicion was evident in his tone. I stopped typing, feeling my cheeks flush. "Why would I be texting Miles?" I asked, trying to mask my embarrassment.

Griffin gave me a knowing look. "You two looked pretty cozy on that blanket," he remarked, causing my embarrassment to deepen. "We were just talking, and that's all. I don't even have his number," I hastily explained. Griffin turned his head, clearly not convinced. "Okay, whatever you say. But can you explain why we need a cover story and what you're doing on your phone?" he pressed on, his curiosity piqued.

I placed my phone back in my pocket and began to articulate, "We can't just stroll into a place and start asking questions without a valid reason. We need a cover story to give us a legitimate purpose for being there. I've been formulating one since we left the house, just in case we ended up visiting the orphanage today." Griffin nodded in comprehension and inquired again about what I was doing on my phone. "I opened my notes app and jotted down some details about the case to enhance the credibility of our cover story," I elaborated. He acknowledged and then questioned our cover story if we were still planning to ask questions about the case. I replied, "Since we're unknown here, I can fabricate anything. I'm thinking of saying that I'm a new student in town, and I need to begin working on a college essay. I'll mention that I saw the missing kids' wanted posters and decided to base my paper on their disappearance." Griffin appeared puzzled. "Would that really work?" he asked. "Generally, when people hear 'college essay,' they hard-ly question anything, so we should be in the clear. The most effective cover blends a bit of truth with the lie," I explained.

As we prepared to begin, Griffin raised a question. "Okay, if that's the story we're sticking with, let's get started. But hold on, if that's your cover, then what's mine?" he asked. As we made our way toward the orphanage, I turned back to re-spond, "You're just my brother that I'm babysitting today, and you're just coming along for the ride." Griffin's expression turned sour as he retorted, "How are you babysitting me when I'm the one looking out for you? I'm not the one with my head in the clouds." I couldn't help but smile as I continued walking, saying, "True, but if you can come up with something better, I would love to hear it." Griffin, visibly frustrated, crossed his arms and muttered to himself. Eventually, he looked up and declared, "Next time, I'll think of something because we don't have time to waste." I chuckled and teased, "Is it that we don't have time to waste, or are you just stumped?" His face turned even redder as he ordered me to shut up.

As I approached the Orphanage, its grandeur reminded me of an old church building. The sprawling main pathway led us to the front entrance, flanked by two imposing two-story red brick buildings with black roofs. These structures were connected by a long red brick one-story building. The first building appeared to be the administrative office, while the second seemed to be where the children resided, evident from the multitude of windows that encased it. Adjacent to the residence was a substantial playground, alive with the joyful sounds of children at play. The parking lot, sparsely dotted with about four cars parked in reserved spots, presumably belonged to the dedicated staff members. Upon reaching the front door, I noticed the imposing presence of large metal double doors securely locked. A sign above a button caught my attention, instructing visitors to "Press Before Entering." This security measure made perfect sense, as protecting the children from strangers was a top priority. It was clear that only authorized individuals were to gain access.

I pressed the worn button next to the imposing metal doors of the building and was met with a jarring buzzing noise. After a moment, a clear, no-nonsense voice belonging to a woman asked, "Who are you here to see?" I quickly explained that I was a student looking to interview the director for a college essay.

There was a tense pause before the woman's voice crackled through the intercom again, granting us permission to see the director. I shot a reassuring smile at Griffin, silently reminding him to stick to our cover story. With a loud click, the heavy metal doors swung open, revealing a dimly lit corridor beyond. As we stepped inside, I steeled myself for the task ahead, knowing it was time to seek the answers I was looking for.

As we entered the room, it felt like stepping into a portal to the past. The walls were painted in a soft shade of pale grey, with a stripe running along the center featuring an intricate pattern of gold and red fish swimming in unison. The room was filled with an array of old paintings, each telling a unique story. Some depicted serene landscapes, showcasing majestic mountain ranges and tranquil lakes, while others portrayed individuals dressed in traditional British attire. As we made our way past a collection of vintage green sofas, we approached the main desk.

Sitting behind the desk was a more prominent woman, perhaps in her late forties. She had short, curly brown hair and fair, milky white skin. She wore round, wire-framed glasses that gave her a studious yet slightly old-fashioned look. Her attire consisted of a green cotton blouse, and she accessorized with a distinctive gold cat necklace. Her piercing gaze made it clear that we had inconvenienced her by entering. In a stern tone, she directed us to ascend the stairs behind her and proceed to the director's office on the second floor, which would be the first door on the right. Although I expressed my gratitude, it was evident that the woman was indifferent to our presence.

Griffin and I ascended the staircase, and upon reaching the second floor, we found it to be much like the first. The walls were adorned with a collection of old paintings, and the familiar pale grey color still dominated the space. As we proceeded two steps forward, a soft, feminine voice beckoned us to enter from our right. I turned to see an office door that had gone unnoticed due to the sheer number of paintings that had captured my attention.

As we entered her office, I couldn't help but notice the modern aesthetic that greeted us. The walls were adorned with a soothing tan-yellow hue and decorated with a diverse collection of landscapes and floral artwork. Positioned against one wall was a sleek L-shaped wooden desk, complemented by a sizable wooden office cabinet. A flourishing fern plant added a touch of greenery beside the window. Gesturing for us to sit, she directed us to the comfortable wooden chairs, each adorned with soft blue cushions that pleasantly surprised me as I settled in. Griffin took a seat in an identical chair beside me. My gaze shifted to the director, who exuded vitality and warmth. She was a middle-aged woman with lustrous brown hair cascading down to her shoulders. Her ears were adorned with elegant gold hoop earrings, and a stunning diamond necklace and wedding ring accentuated her attire—a form-fitting white dress with contrasting black sleeves. Her radiant smile and impeccable physique left a lasting impression. "Hi there, I'm Grace, the director of Hope's Refuge," she introduced herself with a warm smile. "How can I assist you?"

I replied, "Hello, my name is Hazel, and this is my younger brother, Griffin. He's just accompanying me today. We recently relocated here, and I'm entering my final year of high school before heading off to college. I need to write an essay as part of my college application. I came across an article in the newspaper about the ongoing investigation into the missing children. I want to center my essay around honoring their memory and was hoping to ask you some questions about it."

Her warm smile faded as soon as those words left my mouth. It was as if she had aged five years in an instant, the weight of untold stress suddenly etched onto her face. "I took over as director here about eight years ago. It was only a few years after Sophia went missing. I met Linh when I first started here, and she was an amazing little girl, smart as a whip. It really took a toll on me when she disappeared. I know you're looking for information on all of the kids, but Linh is the only one I know," Grace confided.

I asked about Linh's experience here. Grace explained that Linh, like the other children, longed for a family. However, despite coming close to finding one, each potential family would encounter obstacles during the background check process. Grace expressed concern about the families not meeting the organization's standards, leading to disappointment for Linh. She had to reassure Linh that the police were acting in the best interest of the children, although Linh initially believed they were deliberately blocking her adoption. It was a challenging time for Linh, and I had to provide support and comfort during this difficult period.

As I pondered the situation, it occurred to me that Leo might be tampering with the background checks, resulting in none of the families getting approved. It seemed evident that he was fixated on Linh. "I came across information suggesting that Linh ran away and got lost in the woods. However, based on my conversations with some individuals, she didn't seem like the type just to run away. Was there something that prompted her to leave suddenly?" I inquired.

Grace fidgeted in her chair, her brow furrowed as she recounted the events. "Linh never struck me as the runner type, and none of the other missing children did, based on their case files. Linh always seemed content despite not being adopted. Then, one day, I arrived to find her window open, with a makeshift rope made of bed sheets dangling outside. I immediately alerted the authorities and launched a search, but the trail went cold at Stella Creek, just like the others. I can't fathom what led her to run away. Perhaps I overlooked her emotional state. But things have changed now. Every child in our care feels cherished, and they all have potential adoptive families waiting. I won't let my oversight with Linh overshadow the lives of the other children here."

Griffin eagerly raised his hand, reminiscent of a keen student in a classroom hoping to ask a question. Grace responded with a warm smile and called on him to inquire. "I heard that every kid here has a mentor who is also a police officer. Wouldn't Linh's mentor notice if something was off with her? Wouldn't he or she know where she might have gone?" Griffin's question was great, and I appreciated the way he posed it as if we were unaware that Leo was Linh's mentor.

"After Linh disappeared, I made the decision to discontinue the mentor program. It became apparent that many of the children, Linh included, were not comfortable with the program, particularly with her mentor. Linh confided in me about feeling uneasy around him, and while I initially dismissed her concerns as mere stubbornness, I now wonder if he played a role in her departure. I hesitate to make any accusations against him, as he is a respected figure in law enforcement, and I don't want to jump to conclusions about his conduct." Grace replied.

"I guess the police didn't like that since you have to go through them for the background check?" I asked. Grace raised her hand and responded, "We no longer conduct our background checks with the Pinecrest Police Department. We have switched to working with another company and handle everything internally." I was taken aback by her response, as her tone suggested a reluctance to be associated with the police in any way.

I then asked about Linh's and the other kid's mentors, expressing my desire to ask them some questions. Grace's expression turned visibly angry, indicating her unwillingness to dwell on the topic. "Linh's mentor was a man named Leo Davis, and the other four kids were mentored by his father, Robert Davis," she disclosed. This revelation filled in another piece of the puzzle, linking all the kids together through their association with Leo and his father.

With this new information, it seemed that since Grace had terminated the mentor program, there was no longer a specific reason for Leo to target any of the kids here. It appeared that he would have to seek out his next victim elsewhere. However, armed with this knowledge, all that remained was to obtain evidence that he had taken the kids. I speculated that if we could gain access to his house or perhaps investigate the police station, we might uncover the proof we needed.

With a determined look, Griffin raised his hand once more and boldly asked, "I actually have one more question. Do you think that Leo and his dad had something to do with the kids going missing, and that's why you cut ties with them and the police?" As he spoke, I turned in my seat to look at him and noticed that Grace was just as shocked as I was. I couldn't believe he had asked that.

The interview had been going so well, but now I feared that Grace might kick us out and call the police herself.

Grace paused for a moment, took a deep breath, and finally decided to confide in us. "To be honest," she began, choosing her words carefully, "I do believe they had something to do with it, and I mean all of it. But this town is so backward that if I were to voice my concerns, the police would probably try to shut us down. The most I could do was cut ties with them. I don't know for sure that they did anything, but the clues do lead to them and that family. I haven't said this to anyone, but it feels good to get it off my chest. But I must ask that you don't add that in your paper, or it could be horrible for us."

I told Grace not to worry, assuring her that we wouldn't say anything. I thanked her for her time and expressed our appreciation. Her warm smile returned as she told us it was her pleasure and wished me success with my paper and getting into a good school. Griffin and I then got up from our seats and made our way out. As we walked down the steps, we passed by the lady behind the desk. Griffin attempted to wave goodbye to her, but she seemed engrossed in her work and never looked up. Stepping through the double doors, we strolled down the street until we reached the corner of Main Street.

As we walked, I turned to Griffin and said, "That was quite insightful. I thought that last question might get us kicked out. What were you think-ing back there?" Griffin looked down and apologized, expressing his grow-ing frustration with Leo. He felt that Leo was getting away with something just because he was a cop. I reassured him that I understood and shared his feelings. We both agreed that Leo and his family would have to face the con-sequences of their actions. I then pat-ted Griffin on the head and pointed out that the sun was starting to set, suggesting that we should head back to the flower shop.

As we approached the flower shop, a police car caught our attention as it was parked out front. Griffin shot me a desperate look and dashed inside. I hurried in right behind him as he pushed the glass door open. Inside, we were surprised to see my Mom and Detective Leo seated at the display table in the middle of the shop, sipping on tea. They seemed to be sharing a light moment before Griffin's abrupt entrance changed the atmosphere. My Mom stood up, concerned, and asked what was wrong. Before Griffin could speak, I calmly placed my hand on his shoulder and assured them, "We saw the cop car outside and got worried, but we see you were just talking." Leo placed his tea down and walked over to join my Mom. I could sense the anger emanating from Griffin. Leaning down, I urged him to relax and reminded him that we couldn't let Leo know that we were onto him. Gradually, Griffin began to ease, and the tension in his shoulders dissipated.

"I'm sorry to startle you," Leo said. "I was just coming by to see if you all needed help, but Olivia was the only one here. She said you two were out exploring the town, so she invited me to stay for some tea. I should have just used my normal car instead of the police cruiser."

As Leo spoke, my Mom placed her hand on his shoulder and told him it was fine, her voice soothing and calm. I couldn't shake the feeling of discomfort as I watched her touch him. I reminded myself to stay level-headed. Leo and his father were not to be trusted, and soon, they would be exposed and sent away for a long time. Despite my efforts to remain composed, I could feel Griffin, my brother, filling up with rage again.

"Don't you have police work to be doing? Why are you here checking up on our Mom?" Griffin's voice trembled with anger as he confronted Leo.

Ignoring my attempts to console him, Griffin aggressively advanced toward his Leo. "I just got off my shift and thought all of you would be here. I wasn't just coming to see your Mom," Leo explained, raising both hands in a placating gesture. Unmoved, Griffin continued to march forward, his face contorted with fury. Despite being much shorter than Leo, Griffin exuded an intimidating aura, his stance reminiscent of a determined pitbull preparing to confront a much larger adversary.

"Leo, I think you only came here to try and get with my Mom. If you were really here to help, why do you look exactly the same as when we last saw you this morning?" Griffin accused. Leo exchanged a concerned glance with my Mom, who quickly stepped in and reprimanded Griffin, insisting that she and Leo were just friends. "I've heard that one before. But if I'm not mistaken, shouldn't you be out there searching for missing children instead of trying to ask my Mom out on a date?" Griffin challenged.

The atmosphere in the room suddenly shifted to silence when Griffin made his statement. Leo's facial expression clearly displayed his deep-seated anger, and he shot Griffin a menacing glare. Sensing the escalating tension, Mom swiftly positioned herself between the two and, in a stern tone, reprimanded Griffin, emphasizing the importance of his behavior and demanding an apology to Leo. "I'll apologize once he does his job and finds those kids," Griffin retorted defiantly. This response further fueled Mom's fury, and her expression made it seem like Griffin was treading on thin ice.

"I think it's time for me to go anyway. I didn't mean to cause drama. Olivia, I'll see you later. Have a good night, everyone," Leo said. He was starting to make his way out, and my Mom tried to stop him. But then Griffin said, "Good luck with finding those." Leo turned his head back and gave a look that said Griffin would regret saying that, then walked out the door. I was still too stunned to talk because I couldn't believe that Griffin would say all of that. But even with all that confidence to stand up to Leo, my Mom was a different matter. "WHAT HAS GOTTEN INTO YOU?" my Mom yelled so loud I thought the window would shatter. All the courage that Griffin had before just left his body as he slowly turned to face our Mom. Her face was as bright as the sun, and her eyes blazed with fiery fury. I knew Griffin really did it now, and I don't know how he would be able to get out of this one.

Griffin's words cut through the air like a knife. "Mom, Leo is not a good guy. You can't trust him," he said firmly. My Mom's eyes widened in surprise. "What evidence do you have to prove that?" she asked, her voice tinged with concern. Griffin hesitated, avoiding eye contact as he admitted that he didn't have any hard proof. It was a relief that he understood the importance of evidence because, without it, he just looked like a kid making stuff up, but my Mom was still visibly upset.

She sternly warned Griffin that if he ever behaved in such a manner again, he would lose his video game and TV privileges. She even considered making him work in the shop until he was physically exhausted. Despite understanding his discomfort at seeing her talk to another man who wasn't his father, she made it clear that it was no excuse for his behavior. She instructed us to wait in the car while she locked up some things before we could leave. Just then, she remembered that the Wolfkin Farm had called to inform us that our flowers were ready for pickup, and she directed both Griffin and me to go and get them. We both nodded in agreement and walked outside to make our way to the car.

I opened the back door of the car to let Griffin in. Once he was settled, I closed the door and took my place in the front seat. As I adjusted my position, I glanced in the rearview mirror and noticed that Griffin still seemed upset. "Griffin, that was risky. You understand that, don't you?" I remarked. Griffin lifted his head and replied, "You would have done the same. He's a threat, and he's getting too close to our Mom. I couldn't just stand by and do nothing."

I observed him for a moment, as it seemed he was unaware of the implications of his actions. "I'm not referring to that. We've recently discovered that Leo has lost his primary method of targeting children, and now he needs a new approach to identifying a victim. Considering it's the fifth year, he may be actively seeking out someone new, particularly a newcomer to the town who has opposed him. Additionally, isn't it quite coincidental that he is developing a close relationship with a widowed mother who recently lost her husband? It would be relatively simple for him to fabricate a story about a rebellious child who ran away from home due to his mother's new relationship. I suspect he could devise multiple narratives to explain your disappearance," I stated.

Griffin appeared distressed, with a pale face and his head in his hands, expressing regret with the words, "What have I done?" I reassured him that Leo wouldn't come near him. As I finished speaking, our Mom emerged from the flower shop, locked the door, and entered the driver's seat. She started the car, and we began our journey home in silence, sensing her unease. Tomorrow, Griffin and I will be visiting Wolfkin Farm, hoping that the change of scenery will help everyone relax. However, for some reason, I couldn't shake the feeling that something was amiss at Wolfkin Farm. Despite thinking it might be just my imagination, my instincts told me otherwise.

Chapter Eight
A New Puzzle Piece

The following morning, Griffin and I set out for Wolfkin Farm. After a hearty breakfast, my Mom entrusted me with the keys to our only car. She mentioned that she would be staying around the house for the day and suggested that once we picked up the flowers, we should take them to the shop and place them in the walk-in cooler that had been installed the previous day while we were out exploring. It was evident that she was still upset with Griffin, but I assured her that we had everything under control. As I drove, I stole occasional glances at Griffin in the passenger seat to gauge how he was feeling. He still seemed remorseful about yesterday, but I could sense that his intentions were genuine. I hoped that our trip to the farm would provide a welcome distraction for him.

The drive through the countryside was absolutely beautiful. The towering trees, the vibrant green grass, and even the unexpected sighting of a goat all helped to take my mind off the troubling news we received yesterday. While we did manage to piece together some more information, there were still crucial elements of the puzzle that remained elusive. I found myself at a loss, unsure of what our next steps should be. I tentatively suggested that we consider visiting Leo's house to do some discreet investigation, but the potential consequences of being caught weighed heavily on my mind. Besides, we didn't even know where he lived. Another option was to visit the police station, but the thought of getting entangled in further trouble gave me pause. I couldn't fathom a believable cover story for why we would be poking around and asking questions. Perhaps today, we should focus on the task at hand, picking up these flowers and ensuring their safe return to the shop.

As we reached the summit of the towering peak and began our descent into Emerald Valley, the breathtaking sight of the vast, emerald-shaped valley unfolded before us. The lush, vibrant green grass seemed to cascade like a sparkling waterfall down towards the meandering river that flowed directly into the heart of the valley, leading the way to Wolfkin Farm. Towering trees initially obstructed our view of the farm, but we remained confident in our direction. Drawing nearer, the unmistakable sight of the red barn, which also served as a shelter for the farm's vehicles, and the imposing iron gates that guarded the entrance came into view.

Upon reaching the entrance, I activated the intercom, and a lady's voice inquired about our purpose at Wolfkin Farm. I explained that we were there to collect an order for Oliva Torres. The lady confirmed that Ms. Wolfkin was anticipating our arrival and instructed us to drive our car up to the main house, where we would receive further assistance. After expressing my gratitude, the iron gates swung open, allowing us to proceed. Parking the car in the familiar spot from our previous visit, I suggested to

Griffin that we get out and await further instructions. As we stepped out of the car, several workers emerged from the U-shaped building, each carrying multiple buckets filled with exquisite dahlias in an array of captivating colors. It was truly astounding to witness such breathtaking blooms, resembling something out of a masterpiece. After the workers loaded our car with the magnificent flowers, a voice called out to us, prompting us to turn around. We were greeted by Lara Wolfkin, who was elegantly dressed in a white sundress adorned with sunflower prints.

"Hey there, how are you both doing?" Lara inquired with a warm smile. I responded, "We're great, just admiring your beautiful flowers." Lara expressed her gratitude and then asked about the progress of our flower shop. "With this order, I assume you'll be opening soon?" she inquired. "Yes, in just a couple of days. It's been a busy time, but my Mom has been handling most of the work. We're glad to help with picking up this order," I explained. Lara clapped her hands and offered us some freshly made sugar cookies. Before I could respond, Griffin eagerly accepted the offer. We all laughed, and Lara invited us into the main house for some treats.

As we entered through the barn doors, we stepped into a spacious room with tables and chairs stacked in the corners. A large flat-screen TV played in the background, and the huge windows let in plenty of natural light, making the freshly polished wood floors gleam. Lara explained that this was the break room where the workers usually ate lunch. She then excused herself to prepare to-go bags for us, as she knew we were pressed for time with the flowers needing to go into the cooler soon. I asked if I could use the bathroom, and Lara directed me down the hall, pointing out that it would be the second door on the left. I thanked her and made my way down the hall.

As I made my way down the corridor, I was struck by the vibrant and rhythmic sounds of loud music emanating from one of the nearby rooms. The lively beats and cheerful melodies suggested a joyful celebration taking place within. Curious, I approached the door from which the music was emanating and cautiously peeked inside.

To my surprise, I was greeted by a heartwarming scene. Inside the room, several women were tending to a collection of verdant plants, diligently removing dead leaves, trimming the stems, and carefully wrapping them in damp paper towels. Despite the task at hand, their faces were adorned with genuine smiles, and resonant laughter filled the room.

Upon noticing my presence, one of the women swiftly alerted the others, prompting a momentary pause in their activities. With a gracious gesture, the music was lowered, and I couldn't help but feel a tinge of embarrassment at interrupting their harmonious gathering. However, my unease was quickly dispelled as the women collectively greeted me with cheerful "Hola" before erupting into laughter once again.

Among the group, a woman with a warm and inviting demeanor approached me. She stood at a petite stature, her lustrous brown hair elegantly styled in a bun with subtle highlights catching the light. Her caramel-colored complexion exuded a timeless grace, and her mature features hinted at a wealth of life experiences. I estimated her to be in her late thirties, and her captivating presence immediately drew me in.

"Hola, como estas? Mi nombre es Ileana. Puedo ayudarte a encontrar algo?" The lady asked me. My Spanish wasn't that great, but I knew that her name was Ileana. "Hola mi nombre es Hazel. Mi espanol no es tan bueno. Por casualidad hablas ingles? I said. I told her my name was Hazel and that my Spanish wasn't that good. I asked if she spoke English, and luckily, Ileana said yes and asked in English, "Is there something you're looking for?"

"Excuse me, I was actually just looking for the bathroom. I'm here to pick up an order," I explained. Ileana's eyes lit up, and she quickly translated my words to the rest of the ladies. "Oh, are you taking them to a special someone?" she asked, with a mischievous glint in her eyes. I blushed and waved my arms, denying any such implications. I couldn't help but think that if Griffin were here, he would make a joke about me and Miles.

"I'm picking up an order for my Mom. We're opening a flower shop in Pinecrest, and we all just moved here about a week ago. I wish she was here because her Spanish is better than mine. I guess I should have paid more attention to my relatives when they were talking when I was young," I chuckled. Ileana asked me where my Mom was from, and I told her that our family is from El Salvador. Ileana and the other ladies all clapped with excitement. "All of my sisters and I here are from El Salvador. Let me introduce you from left to right. We have Liliana, Krisia, Maria, Jobana, Linda, China, Yesenia, Yamileth, Glendy, Eli, and finally Ali. We've all been working here for the past 18 years. Is it just you and your Mom?" Ileana inquired.

"No, my brother is here too. His name is Griffin. He's actually in the other room with Lara," I replied. All of the ladies' faces changed from looks of joy to looks of concern. "How old is your brother?" Ileana asked. I started to worry as I noticed the mood in the room shift. "He's 12 years old," I answered. Suddenly, one of the ladies stood up and started speaking in Spanish so fast that I couldn't understand. Ileana quickly told her to calm down and turned to me, saying, "You need to get your brother and leave here and never come back."

"Wait, hold on, what's going on? Is my brother in danger?" I asked anxiously. Ileana put a finger to her lips, signaling for me to be quiet. "This place is evil, and your brother is not safe, especially around Ms. Wolfkin," Ileana whispered urgently. I lowered my voice and asked her what she meant by the place being evil. Ileana glanced around to ensure no one was listening before she began to speak.

"We've been living here for a long time, right behind the farm on the other side of the tree line. About three years after we moved here, the big chimney in the back started spewing black smoke that covered the entire sky. We thought Ms. Wolfkin was just making fertilizer or something, as we heard she makes it in the basement using fire. But five years later, Liliana and I stayed late to finish an order for the next day. As we were leaving, the chimney started spewing black smoke again, and we heard a child screaming and crying. Terrified, we ran home and told everyone what we heard, but Jorge advised us to keep quiet about it."

"Five more years passed, and the chimney started up again. This time, all my sisters and I decided to go investigate. As we approached the main house, we heard a little girl screaming, and we were so frightened that we all ran away. The noise seemed to be coming from the basement. We know the chimney will start again this year, and we don't know what's happening. You need to get your brother out of here because this place is not safe," Ileana explained with a worried look on her face.

After hearing what Ileana had to say, my mind was filled with new puzzle pieces. They've been living here for 18 years, which rounds down to 15. Every five years, they witnessed the chimney starting, and for the past ten years, they heard children screaming when it started. Now, with this being the fifth year, they know the chimney will start again soon. It's a pattern of 5 years, every five years, and the sound of children that they could see. If I'm piecing this together correctly, then I may have just figured out where the five missing children from Pinecrest went. It's either an unbelievable coincidence, and there's something else going on, or I've just uncovered our real kidnapper.

"Ileana, do you know about the five missing orphans from Pinecrest?" I asked urgently, my voice filled with concern. She shook her head, a troubled expression crossing her features. I suspected that Lara would keep her workers in the dark about such unsettling news. "Ileana, why haven't you reported this to anyone?" I inquired, hoping to understand her perspective. Ileana hesitated, her gaze shifting to the skin on her hand as if searching for the right words. "When people like me try to seek help, it never turns out the way we hope," she confessed, her voice tinged with resignation. I felt a pang of empathy, realizing the harsh reality she faced. "Why stay here, Ileana? Isn't there another farm you could work at?" I pressed gently, concern evident in my tone. "I stay because of my family. We rely on the work, and I need to provide for them. I can't leave with nowhere to go and no means to support them," Ileana explained, her words reflecting the weight of her responsibilities. I nodded, understanding the depth of her commitment. "Ileana, I'm a detective. I uncover mysteries and find the truth. I'm going to expose this place and what Lara Wolfkin is up to. When I uncover the truth, I will report it and ensure Lara faces the consequences," I stated firmly, hoping to offer Ileana some reassurance. Ileana's eyes widened in surprise, and then she embraced me tightly. As we drew apart, she expressed her gratitude, her voice filled with emotion. "Thank you. I couldn't bear it if nothing was done," she murmured. "But when I do this, the farm will shut down, and you all will be out of a job," I pointed out, concerned about the impact of my actions on Ileana and her family. "I will never leave voluntarily, but if this place is exposed for the evil that takes place here, me and my family will accept that fate. We are survivors; we will find a way. Thank you, Hazel, for listening to me," Ileana said, her resolve shining through. "No, Ileana, thank you for confiding in me. I promise your trust won't be in vain," I assured her, feeling a renewed determination to bring the truth to light, and we shared one last heartfelt hug.

I dashed down the dimly lit and eerily quiet hallway, my heart pounding in my chest, desperately hoping that Griffin was still alone. I had been gone for longer than I had anticipated, and time was of the essence. As I burst into the break room, relief washed over me as I saw Griffin sitting by himself in a worn-out chair near the door. His expression was a mix of concern and confusion as he glanced up at me, the faint light casting long shadows across the room.

I hurried over to him, trying to mask the urgency in my voice, and asked if he was okay. He assured me that he was fine and mentioned that he was waiting for Lara to return. With a sense of growing panic, I pleaded with him to stall for me. I couldn't explain the situation fully, but I begged him to tell Lara that I was unwell and still in the bathroom. After nodding in understanding, I gave him a quick hug and stressed the importance of not leaving with Lara until I returned. Leaving him with more questions than answers, I raced back down the hall to find the bathroom.

Once inside, I noticed a window and felt a surge of hope. I locked the door, approached the window, and cautiously peered outside to ensure that no one was nearby. Satisfied that the coast was clear, I carefully unlatched the window and pushed it open, the cool evening air rushing in. I climbed out onto the narrow ledge, the rough texture of the bricks scraping against my fingertips as I held on, careful not to make any noise that might draw attention.

I made my way around the building, staying close to the walls to remain hidden from view. As I turned the corner, my eyes fell upon a set of imposing double doors next to the chimney leading down to the basement. It was time to investigate and uncover the truth.

Approaching the doors, I was disheartened to find a large, ancient-looking padlock securing them. However, luck was on my side when I spotted a small window near the bottom. Lying flat on the ground, I peered through the window and, realizing that my view was limited, took out my phone to record the scene. With time ticking away, I needed to capture everything I could for later review.

Inside the basement, I observed a seemingly ordinary sight: a dirt floor, a few shelves with nondescript burlap sacks, perhaps the fertilizer mentioned in Lara's conversations. But then, something on the floor caught my eye. Struggling to discern what it was, I zoomed in and enabled autofocus on my phone. As the image came into focus, I was stunned. The ground seemed to fall away beneath me as I stood up and sprinted back to the bathroom window.

Re-entering the bathroom, I hastily closed the window, flushed the toilet, and turned on the sink for a few seconds before rushing back into the hallway. My eyes fell upon Griffin and Lara sitting at a table, enjoying some cookies. I took a moment to compose myself, trying to conceal the panic that threatened to consume me.

Lara's concerned voice cut through the tension as she inquired about Hazel's well-being. "Hazel, are you feeling better? Griffin told me you were ill. I have some tea that can help upset stomachs if you want," she said, her eyes filled with genuine concern. Despite the urgency of the situation, I maintained my composure. I couldn't afford to tip off Lara or give her any reason to suspect that something was amiss. "No, thank you. I will be fine. I did just get a text from my Mom saying we need to get the flowers in the cooler as fast as possible. It was nice seeing you again, and thank you for the cookies," I replied, mustering a polite smile. Griffin rose from his seat and expressed his gratitude to Lara for the delicious cookies. "Well, I'm sorry you have to leave so soon, but please do come back, and I hope your mom will join you next time," Lara said warmly as we said our goodbyes. We made our way to the car, and Griffin began to question me about what was going on. I urged him to wait until we were away from the farm before catching him up. Griffin's worried expression mirrored my own fear. My sole focus now was to put as much distance between us and the flower farm. As we approached the iron gates, they swung open, and I drove through. Once we made it to the top of the valley, I hit the gas. My determination overrode Griffin's pleas to slow down; tunnel vision consumed me as I gunned the engine, craving the safety of distance from the farm.

After driving a couple of miles, I felt the need to pull over and take a moment to collect my thoughts. The weight of everything that had been happening hit me all at once, and I found it hard to catch my breath. Griffin, sensing my distress, placed a reassuring hand on my shoulder and encouraged me to relax and share what was troubling me. I could see the concern in his eyes, and it made me realize how much I had unsettled him. I took a few deep breaths and managed to compose myself. Sitting back in my seat, I decided to confide in him. I recounted everything that had transpired - from what Ileana had told me to sneaking out of the window and venturing to the basement to even capturing a video of what I had witnessed through the window. I explained that what I had seen had compelled me to hurry back for our safety. Griffin inquired about what I had seen in the basement, prompting me to show him the video on my phone. As he watched, I noticed a growing sense of panic on his face, and he asked me if what he saw was true. I told him yes. It was clear that his mind was racing as we both reacted to what we had seen. In the dimly lit back corner of the basement, a dusty red ribbon adorned with a golden eagle caught our attention - the very same red ribbon that Linh used to wear in her hair.

Chapter Nine
The Truth Unfolds

I was completely unprepared to find myself standing in the basement, facing Detective Leo. It was as if everything had gone terribly wrong. I instinctively backed away as Leo approached me, pleading for him to stay away. Ignoring my pleas, Leo took out his phone and began typing, clearly communicating with someone. "Who are you talking to, and what are you doing?" I demanded, but Leo remained focused on his phone. When he finished, he calmly returned his phone to his pocket and locked eyes with me. His words sent a shiver down my spine: "You should have heeded your mother's warning." Fear gripped me as I tried to comprehend what Leo might do next. "Why are you here, and how did you even know I was in the basement?" I asked, desperate for any answers.

He wore a sly grin on his face as he chuckled softly to himself. "Regarding your first question, I'll wait for Lara to arrive before answering. As for your second question, I installed a motion sensor on the basement door, which alerts my phone whenever someone enters. I initially suspected Lara might be down there, but after seeing her and your brother in the rose garden, I realized something was up. You're quite resourceful, but it doesn't matter now," Leo declared. I didn't want to reveal that it was mere chance that led me to come downstairs, nor did I want to expose that Ileana and her sisters had shared the eerie stories associated with this farm. I scanned the surroundings for any possible way to evade him, but he had sealed off the sole exit.

I noticed a small red light out of the corner of my eye and realized that my phone was still recording. Leo hadn't seen my phone yet and was complete-ly unaware that I was live-streaming. In a desperate attempt to attract at-tention, I kept Leo engaged in conver-sation, hoping that someone watch-ing would call the police. "What's happening here, Leo? Why did you take those kids, and why are their clothes hidden in a chest behind a brick wall?" I asked, trying to sound brave despite the fear gnawing at me. Leo casually waved his hand and in-formed me that we were waiting for Lara to arrive with my brother. "She should be here with your brother any second now," he said nonchalantly. As the fear slowly subsided, anger be-gan to build up inside me. "Don't you dare lay a hand on Griffin," I demand-ed sternly. Leo laughed callously and replied, "Well, that depends on how your brother behaves."

A moment later, I could hear Grif-fin's tense voice as he confronted Lara, "You better not have hurt my sister." It struck me how similar we were, both fiercely protective of each other's well-being. As Lara and Grif-fin descended into the basement, Griffin spotted me and hurried over, enveloping me in a comforting em-brace. Concern etched on his face, he asked if I was alright. Assuring him that I was unharmed, I turned to ad-dress the pressing issues at hand. My gaze met Lara's, who seemed to regard our presence in her basement with thinly veiled disapproval. "Now that Lara is here, are you going to tell me what's going on?" I inquired. A silent exchange passed between Lara and Leo as if they were silently deciding who would speak first. "Well, since it's my farm, I guess I will explain," Lara eventually offered. She paused, taking a deep breath before continuing. "Cultivating plants is an arduous task. It requires significant effort, and the outcome isn't always as expected. I grew weary of the unpredictable nature of it all and sought out alternative methods. While commercial fertilizers like Osmocote were effective, I craved something more.

I stumbled upon an ancient tome that discussed the spiritual connection between flowers and our souls. It dawned on me – what if I could imbue the flowers with more than just our soul's resonance? What if I could infuse them with something greater?" Griffin and I exchanged perplexed glances. "Where is this going, and what does it have to do with the kids?" I pressed.

Lara flashed a smile and went on, "Hazel, have you ever considered making your own fertilizer? The process involves subjecting it to high temperatures while simultaneously mixing the ingredients. For instance, I would take this Osmocote, toss bags of it into the furnace, and then incorporate the other components. I trust you can envision the direction I'm heading in. Let me break it down for you: I required something more potent than a soul wavelength and something capable of igniting alongside my Osmocote. So, Hazel, as an excellent aspiring detective, what surpasses a soul?"

I carefully considered the situation and envisioned the scenario in my mind. Leo, Leo's father, and Lara took the children from the local orphanage and brought them to the basement. The basement housed a large furnace and a hidden wall where the children's clothes were stored to conceal their presence. As I pieced together the details, one crucial element remained unresolved. I glanced at the shelf filled with burlap bags of grey ash, and suddenly, everything fell into place. The long and heart-wrenching puzzle was finally complete.

"You burned the children to Ash to mix them in with your fertilizer!" I said

Griffin yelled, "That's crazy." Lara applauded and chuckled, "You are such a clever girl. Yes, that's exactly what I've been doing for the past 30 years, and I was getting away with it until Leo's father fell ill and passed away. However, the new director at the orphanage interfered and ended the mentor program. I was worried about how we would keep the supplies going, but then Leo came up with an idea that actually seemed to work after all."

Griffin inquired, "What idea?" Leo turned his head, wearing a disappointed expression. "I thought you were clever too, but I suppose it's only your sister. I bet you've already figured it out, haven't you, Hazel," Leo remarked. Griffin turned to me, looking perplexed. I was just as bewildered; I had no clue what he was referring to. "Oh, Hazel, you've come this far, and you still haven't figured it out? Alright, here's a hint. Do you really think it was a coincidence that I met your mom at the police station?" Leo asked. It was at that moment that everything clicked in my mind, and I exclaimed, "You knew we were moving here, and you sought us out from the beginning." Leo confirmed, "Bingo. Yes, I knew a widow and her children would be moving here soon, and I noticed that she submitted paperwork to open a flower shop in town. It was only a matter of time before I made our paths cross. It's very convenient that city hall and the police station are housed in the same building." Realization struck - Leo had been pursuing us all along, a fact that we had failed to recognize. "Alright, you've demonstrated what a sick individual you are, but I still don't comprehend how you benefit from this," I insisted. Leo glanced at Lara, and she motioned as if to signal him to share the truth. "Well, I suppose it doesn't matter now. I am her son," Leo disclosed.

Griffin and I were in utter disbelief as we tried to process the bombshell Leo had just dropped on us. "So, your father, Robert Davis, and Lara were actually married?" Griffin inquired, hoping to clarify the situation. Leo shook his head, replying, "No, they never tied the knot, but they were together. They transformed this humble farm into a thriving multi-million dollar company. After my father passed away, I was determined to protect his legacy. I made sure my mother had everything she needed, even if it meant having children to secure the family's future," Leo explained, a sly grin stretching across his face.

Leo's true nature was finally revealed as that of an evil man driven solely by greed. It was clear that his parents had played a role in shaping him into the monstrous figure he had become. The unexpected turn of events left us grappling with the daunting challenge of finding a way out of our predicament. I couldn't help but voice my lingering questions, "Since you're being honest, I do have two more questions. Why every five years and why only take kids who are under the age of 13?"

Lara, taking a step forward, began to explain, "When I finish producing the fertilizer, it typically lasts for about five years before we need to replenish our stocks. As for the children, before they reach the age of 13, their souls are still in the process of developing. They are rich with a variety of emotions as they have not yet fully formed their identities. Using someone like you, Hazel, whose soul is more mature, may result in the loss of certain flavors. However, rest assured that even if I cannot turn you into fertilizer, you will still serve a purpose in my compost beds," Lara said with her eyes closed, though I could still feel the piercing intensity of her cold gaze.

"Alright, we don't have much time," Lara declared, striding purposefully towards the furnace. With a determined push of a red button on its side, the dormant machine roared to life, instantly raising the room's temperature by a startling 100 degrees. "Are you really going to do this now, rather than waiting until later?" I questioned. Leo sighed, shifting his weight from one foot to the other. "Our original plan went out the window. You and Lara need to stay here. Lara will work her magic, and I'll take your car down the road and make it look like you both were in an acci-dent. No one will be the wiser, and your mom will be so distraught she might decide to move to Canada," he explained. "But what about explaining our absence from the car?" Griffin inquired. Leo flashed a sly smile. "I'll use part of the same story we used before. I'll say the animals got to you before we arrived," he replied confidently. Suddenly, Lara stepped closer, and I instinctively warned her to stay away from my brother. Leo then reached into his pocket and produced a small, black, rectangular box. With a quick press on its side, a loud zapping noise accompanied by blue sparks crackled from the device. I realized Leo had a taser, and with a chilling calmness, he presented it to Lara. "You have a choice: you can either cooperate willingly, or we can resort to option B," she threatened, her finger firmly holding down the taser's button.

As my mind raced, we ended up getting more than we had expected - a full-blown confession, all of which was live-streamed without Lara and Leo noticing. When Leo asked for my keys, I had no choice but to hand them over to him. We were backed against the wall, and there was no room for a fight. As Leo whispered something to Lara and left the basement, it suddenly became just the three of us. The panic in my brother's face mirrored my own fears, and I couldn't think of a way out of this nightmare. All I could think was, is this the end?

Chapter Ten
Case Closed

I strained to survey the area, desperately searching for an escape route or a way to signal one of the workers outside. The fateful sound of the lock clicking shut as Leo left confirmed that we were now trapped underground with Lara brandishing a taser. She gestured for Griffin to approach the furnace, but I moved to shield him. Warning us not to defy her, Lara insisted that we comply with her commands.

The room was becoming increasingly hazy, and I became aware that the intense heat was causing dizziness. My vision was beginning to blur, and the sweat dripping into my eyes stung so much that I hesitated to shut them. Glancing at Griffin, I noticed he was soaked in sweat, appearing as though the oppressive heat was affecting his mental state, too. It was truly miserable for both of us, barely clinging on. In contrast, Lara seemed completely unaffected by the heat.

"Are you not affected by the heat?" I inquired of Lara. "When you've been doing this for a while, you build up a tolerance. Now, Griffin, move in front of the furnace door," Lara ordered.

"Yeah, that's not happening," Griffin stated firmly. Undeterred, Lara insisted that he didn't have a choice. As the gravity of the situation settled in, I was hit with a realization that it felt like a risky move. But at that point, there was nothing to lose, so I decided to take the plunge. I turned and knelt down to embrace my brother. Despite Lara's objections, I was determined that if it might be the final time I saw my brother, I had to give him a hug. I held Griffin close and murmured in his ear, "Get her to step in front of the door." After a moment, Griffin released me and, wearing an expression of exhaustion, gave me a subtle nod.

Griffin hesitantly shuffled over to the looming furnace door, where he could feel the intense heat radiating from within. Standing in front of the imposing door, Griffin's chest swelled with determination. Just as he was about to take the final step, he turned to Lara and asked, "How should I position myself?" Lara appeared puzzled. "Simply stand in front of the door and go through," she responded. Griffin hesitated, "I don't want to make any mistakes, and then you'll take it out on my sister. Can't you just demonstrate for me?" Irritated, Lara walked over to him, swung the door open, and a scorching wave of heat struck their faces. "Just stand here and step in, hurry up," she insisted.

With the last ounce of bravery coursing through my veins, I dashed towards Lara and forcefully propelled her through the door. Gripping the door handle, I attempted to slam it shut, only to be met with a searing heat that singed my skin. Despite Lara's frantic attempts to open the door, I strained with every fiber of my being to keep it closed. As my strength waned, I struggled to maintain my grip. In that critical moment, Griffin hurled himself against the door with tremendous force.

As my brother and I struggled to shut the door, we collapsed to the

ground in exhaustion. I was horri-
fied to see the extent of the burns on
my brother's skin, and when I looked
at my own hands and arms, I was
shocked to discover that most of my
skin had been seared away. We were
both in shock, unable to move, as
chilling sounds paralyzed us.

Lara's piercing screams echoed
from the other side of the door as she
desperately called out for Leo. Griffin and I lay frozen, unable to move,
as the sound of her voice slowly faded away, leaving an eerie silence in
its wake. I struggled to push myself
to my feet, my heart pounding in my
chest, and made my way over to a
control panel where a bright red but-

ton with the words "emergency stop" caught my eye.

I pushed my shoulder against the button, and the deafening roar of the furnace subsided as the scorching heat dissipated. As the room quickly cooled, I turned to see Griffin on the floor, his eyes wide with shock and his hands shaking from the searing pain of the burns. The sudden silence seemed to amplify the intensity of the situation. In a corner of the room, I spotted a first aid kit and hurried over to it. Opening the box, I found a large bottle of burn cream and rushed back to Griffin's side. Pouring the soothing cream over his burns, I gently massaged it in, offering him some relief from the agony. As he began to relax, I carefully tended to my own burns, feeling the weight of our actions settle heavily upon me. It was a risky move that had paid off, but the toll it had taken on us was undeniable. What have we done?

After what seemed like an eternity sitting on the dirty, pale floor of the basement, Griffin and I turned to each other. I locked eyes with him, and my vision grew hazy as I noticed the tears welling up. His eyes were also filled with tears as they streamed down his cheeks. We inched closer to each other, finding solace in our shared tears. The ordeal we had just endured was far too harrowing to articulate, but the relief I felt knowing my brother was safe outweighed everything else. Despite being trapped in this basement, we were both alive, and at that moment, that was more than enough.

As the tears subsided, I reassured him that everything would be okay. He was still crying, expressing his love and gratitude for saving his life. I reminded him that we saved each other and promised to always be there for him. He echoed the same sentiment, acknowledging that we were partners and vowed to always have each other's back. Helping him to his feet, I planted a kiss on the top of his head and advised him to continue applying burn cream while I brainstormed our escape plan.

After realizing that my phone was still recording, I made my way to the basement window and was astonished to see that my phone was still live streaming. I looked at the viewer count and was shocked to see that over 100 million people were tuned in. My phone was inundated with messages expressing concern for our well-being, hailing me and Griffin as heroes, and urging us to contact the authorities. It suddenly dawned on me why those messages were pouring in. I reassured the viewers that we were safe and expressed gratitude to them for continuing to watch, as their presence provided us with witnesses. With a sense of relief, I terminated the stream, realizing that it was sheer luck that had led to this situation, but also acknowledging that we now had an audience that could corroborate our story and attest to Leao and Lara's confession.

I hastily dialed 911, and with a surge of relief, the operator picked up. Frantically, I informed her that I was Hazel Torres and my brother Griffin was trapped in a basement. However, before I could finish, the operator already knew what was happening. She reassured me, "Hazel, we've received multiple reports about the situation. We've closely monitored the entire live stream and witnessed Leo and Lara's admission. We also observed your plea for help, and rest assured that you and Griffin are not in trouble. Our officers are en route to Wolfkin Farm and have successfully apprehended Leo Davis. He was found trying to escape in your mother's car. We've already contacted your mother, and she is accompanying the police to your location. They'll be with you shortly, so stay calm. A medical team is also on their way to tend to any injuries. Hazel, you did an outstanding job. You should be proud that you and your brother are safe."

After thanking the operator, I explained that I needed to focus on my brother and said goodbye. The understanding operator wished us well, and we ended the call.

I placed my hand on Griffin's shoulder as he gazed at the furnace, lost in thought. "Are we bad people, Hazel?" he asked, his voice filled with doubt. I moved closer to him, trying to reassure him. "We are not bad people, Griffin. We are survivors. And now that this is over, we can take solace in the fact that we have brought the truth to light. Tommy, Emily, Carlos, Sophia, and Linh can now rest knowing the truth is out there," I said. Griffin nodded in understanding. "It's hard to believe that our first case together turned out to be so extreme.

But despite the way it ended, I loved every moment of working with you, Hazel. I now understand why you and Dad love this stuff," he added. I couldn't help but smile as I gently ran my hand through his hair.

A jarring noise echoed from the other side of the basement door, followed by a man's urgent shout claiming to be the police. He asked if we were still inside, to which I responded affirmatively, mentioning that the door was locked. He instructed us to move away from the door. Griffin and I stepped back just as we heard a sharp popping sound, followed by a metallic clatter as a lock hit the ground. The door swung open, flooding the room with blinding light, temporarily obscuring our vision. I exchanged a reassuring smile with my brother as we cautiously made our way through the doorway, uttering, "Finally, this case is closed."

Epilogue

As I lounged at home on the cozy couch, engrossed in the latest news update, my mind wandered back over the past couple of months and the whirlwind of events that had unfolded. Griffin and I had been hailed as town heroes for exposing the truth about Leo and his father's cover-up. Wolfkin Farm had shut down, but to our relief, another flower farm had acquired the property and retained all the staff. Ileana and her sisters still had their jobs, and I made it a point to visit them occasionally. Ileana always treated us to her delicious pupusas whenever we dropped by.

My mother kept apologizing for inadvertently getting involved with Leo, but we assured her that everything was alright. Meanwhile, we pressed on with the grand opening of the flower shop, which received overwhelming support from the community. After school, I started pitching in at the shop to assist my mom, and Griffin found his place on the school's debate team alongside his new best friend, Lucas. Griffin quickly settled in at school while I tended to keep to myself. However, I did strike up a great friendship with Miles, who just waltzed in with a bowl of popcorn. We began spending more time together after we wrapped up the case. He expressed his gratitude for our role in exposing Leo's involvement in the disappearances and thanked me for solving his friend Linh's case.

"Why are you tuned in to the news? I thought we were going to watch 'Knives Out,' the mystery movie. I'm curious to see what movie you hold in high esteem," Miles chimed in. I snatched up some more pop-corn. "We will, but I just wanted to catch up on the current events," I replied. Just then, the news anchor announced, "Over the past few days, a series of home burglaries have plagued Princecrest Falls, and the stolen items will surprise you. We'll be right back after these messages." My heart raced, the hairs on my arms stood on end, and a familiar sense of anticipation washed over me. A new case had surfaced, and it was time for Hazel and Griffin to leap into action.

Acknowledgemen

I want to acknowledge someone who played a significant role in helping me write this book. She was my primary source of flower knowledge and helped me choose the location for the story. She is like a sister to me and owns a flower farm where she grows flowers and turns them into beautiful flower jewelry. I want to express my gratitude to Lara Jackson, the owner of Wolfsong Farm. Although she is nothing like the character Lara in our story "Hazel & Griffin," I based the appearance of the character Lara Wolfkin on Lara Jackson. Her flower knowledge has been invaluable to the making of this book. Here is some information if you would like to know more about Lara Jackson and Wolfsong Flowers.

Lara is the owner and operator of Wolfsong Flowers. WF is a woman-owned, small business located just outside of Athens, GA. (about an hour East of Atlanta, GA). It is both a flower farm and an art studio. I specialize in flower preservation, specifically wedding flowers and bridal bouquets. I also grow and locally sell seasonal specialty cut flowers. Lastly, I make jewelry with preserved flowers grown on our flower farm.

Please visit Wolfsong Flowers at w ww.wolfsongflowers.com

I would also like to thank my coworkers Ileana, Liliana, Krisia, Maria, Jobana, Linda, China, Yesenia, Yamileth, Glendy, Eli, Ali, Sophia, and Jorge for allowing me to use their names as characters in the story.

About the author

Atticus Blackwood is a talented author hailing from Athens, GA, whose literary works seamlessly blend the genres of realistic fiction, mystery, and supernatural elements, creating a captivating and unique reading experience. His stories transport both young adult and adult readers to immersive worlds that skillfully merge the ordinary with the extraordinary, weaving together suspense and intrigue. Atticus is known for his writing style, which effortlessly combines a casual and approachable tone with expert storytelling prowess, allowing readers to deeply connect with his well-crafted characters and enthralling narratives. Fueled by a deep-seated passion for creating compelling adventures, Atticus has the remarkable ability to transform everyday moments into extraordinary tales that continue to resonate with readers long after they've finished reading.